BOOKS BY CHARLENE TALBOT

A Home With Aunt Florry
The Great Rat Island Adventure

The
Great Rat Island
Adventure

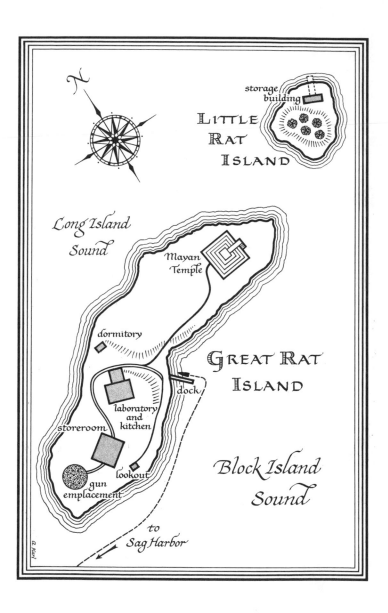

CHARLENE JOY TALBOT

The
Great Rat Island
Adventure

DRAWINGS BY RUTH SANDERSON

Atheneum · 1977 · New York

LIBRARY OF CONGRESS CATALOGING IN PUBLICATION DATA

Talbot, Charlene Joy.
The Great Rat Island adventure.

SUMMARY: A young boy accompanies his preoccupied
ornithologist father on a summer expedition to study
terns on an island sanctuary and finds himself involved
in a dangerous adventure when a hurricane strikes.
[1. Hurricanes—Fiction.   2. Islands—Fiction.
3. Fathers and sons—Fiction]   I. Sanderson, Ruth.
II. Title.
PZ7.T1418Gr   [Fic]   77-1055
ISBN 0-689-30596-6

Published simultaneously in Canada by
McClelland & Stewart, Ltd.
Manufactured in the United States of America by
The Book Press, Brattleboro, Vermont
Designed by David Rogers and Mary M. Ahern
First Edition

For Brian and Daniel Weber

Contents

The
Great Rat Island
Adventure

I

"He doesn't want me, does he?"

Joel Curtis shifted his schoolbooks to his other hand and unlocked the downstairs door. He began to ascend the wooden stairs that went up and back, one flight beyond the other, until on the fourth floor you found yourself looking out the rear window. "Our stairway to the stars," his mother called it, but it was a long climb.

Joel lived in a part of New York City that consisted of old warehouses, many of which artists had taken over. The empty floors, known as lofts, were so big you could live in one end and paint or make things in the other. Joel's mother designed clothes.

As Joel unlocked the door to the loft, he heard his mother in her workroom, talking on the phone. She sounded angry.

"Oh, *I* stuff him with junk food, do I?" she was saying. "All right, take him for two months and see what you can do."

She must be quarreling with his father. Now that they were divorced, they did their quarreling over the phone. He knew he shouldn't be listening, but after all they were talking about him. He moved silently toward the kitchen.

His mother's voice echoed in the big space. "Marshall. . . . Please take him!"

It sounded as if his father didn't want to.

"How can I take him to Europe?" Joel's mother argued. "You can't drag a kid around Europe! How could I get anything accomplished? . . . Put him on a tour bus? Don't be ridiculous! You don't consider his needs at all."

Joel cringed inside himself.

"I'll tell you what he needs, he needs his father! He *wouldn't* eat so much if you spent more time with him."

Pause.

"It's not right! You *agreed* to take him for two months during the summer. This year you've got to do it!"

Another pause.

"You can assign one of your assistants to look after him, if you can't be bothered."

Joel slammed the refrigerator door, but the well-bred box only closed with an aloof click.

His mother's voice sharpened. "He's home! I'll talk to you tomorrow."

Joel heard her steps cross the bare workroom floor, and then she came into the kitchen. She saw him with the jar of peanut butter and made a face.

"So you've been here awhile," she said.

"Not long," Joel muttered.

4

She accepted the fact that he had been eavesdropping, because she said in an exasperated voice, "Well, you know I have to go to Europe. I don't just *have* to, I want to. I want to see what's happening in the Paris fashion houses. Your father should understand."

"He doesn't want me, does he?" Joel took a quick glance at his mother's face.

She sighed. "Oh . . . he thinks he doesn't, because he'll have to look after you. Well, he barely looks after himself! But he's hardly seen you for two years. He doesn't understand that an eleven-year-old doesn't need much looking after. He ought to spend some time with you, and vice-versa. Even if I could take you, sweetie, I'd still insist you ought to be with him."

"What if he says no?"

"He won't say no."

"Where's he going, anyway?"

"To a small island. At the far end of Long Island."

"Is it his vacation?"

"When did your father ever take a vacation? He enjoys his work too much. Well, I don't mean to criticize him. The island belongs to the Institute of Coastal Science. A lot of birds nest there. He's going to be doing . . ." She shrugged. ". . . what ornithologists do."

"Why can't I stay with Grandma and Grandpa?"

"You know Grandma hasn't been well. Besides, you *ought* to be with your father."

"It was nice on Staten Island last summer," Joel said wistfully. "I have some friends out there."

"But Staten Island's still the city, darling. On a *small*

5

island you can go swimming and fishing and—whatever."
She gave him a friendly smile. "Think how safe you'll
be. I won't have to worry about a thing."

In his room Joel picked a science fiction magazine
from his bookcase and chose a candy bar from his hoard.
As he reread two stories and ate the candy bar, his worry
about summer retreated. Among the galaxies things
happened to other people and came out all right.

Coming home from school next day, Joel remembered
that his mother was going to talk to his father again.
His stomach felt troubled, and he decided a bag of corn
chips would taste good. He counted his change to see
if he had enough to buy the large size.

When he reached home, he didn't have any trouble
sneaking in the corn chips. His mother was on the phone
again with his father.

Joel made for his room, tucked the bag of chips
under his pillow, then headed for the workroom. Maybe
his father would want to talk to him.

His mother saw him and smiled. "Joel's just come in,"
she said to the phone. "I thought you'd call earlier."
The next thing she said, in her business-type voice was:
"I've been thinking it over, too, Marshall. Some of his
friends are going to a camp near Lake George—"

Joel watched her face. What was his father saying?

His mother said, "It costs around a thousand a month."

Joel didn't have to guess his father's reply to that.
He could hear the squawk. His mother held the phone
away from her ear and grinned at Joel.

"For heaven's sake, Marshall, I should think you'd

want to spend some time with your son!

"He won't *get* sick. If he does, don't you have any female scientists who can look after him?"

This time the noises from the receiver sounded like growls.

"No women?" Joel's mother sounded surprised. "How do you get away with such discrimination? Anyway, I daresay there are *men* capable of looking after a boy, if you can't face it . . .

"Well, it's either that or camp . . .

"You will? Marshall, believe me, you'll be glad! Do you want to talk to him? Oh. I'll tell him. . . You'll be going the first of May. . . Yes, I understand. I'll get his clothes ready. School's out June twenty-ninth. Okay, good enough. 'Bye." She hung up the phone.

"Didn't he want to talk to me?" Joel asked.

"He couldn't, honey. He was due at a meeting."

Joel shoved out his lower lip. Grown-ups did what they wanted. If they wanted to talk to people, they could.

"Well," she said. "I guess you heard. He's going to take you."

"He doesn't want to," Joel stated.

"Darling, your father's only interested in Science. For him, Science means birds. He just isn't interested in people. You're old enough to understand that now. Look, he spent a year in Brazil doing research on Brazilian birds, and what did he do for a vacation? He went to New Guinea to spend a year cataloging New Guinea birds."

Joel responded to his mother's smile, but what she

7

said didn't help. He was glad his father liked his work, but fathers were supposed to like their children, too.

He climbed into the top bunk with a new sci-fi magazine—a loan from his friend Paul. He was glad he'd bought the corn chips. He guessed he'd need them.

How big was the island where he was going? Big enough to get lost on? Who *would* look after him if he got sick? His father's work always took him where there were no towns or people. Joel could remember the weekends before his father went to Brazil. Long, endless, tiring walks, sometimes with students along. They got tired, too, and lagged behind and groaned. Of course, he was older now, better able to cope, but he was also fat. Which seemed to annoy everybody.

He sighed and finished the corn chips, determined to forget what was going to happen until he had to remember.

From time to time Joel did think about the summer with his father, but in the beginning it was only April. Even his father wasn't going to move to the island until May first. To count terns' eggs, his mother said. Terns were birds. The island was called Great Rat.

At the end of April his father telephoned. After he got to the island they wouldn't be able to talk to him, he said. The island didn't have a telephone. A boat stopped once a week to deliver mail and groceries. It sounded as far away as New Guinea.

The end of June was still weeks away when Joel's mother took him uptown to buy a sleeping bag.

8

The store was like none he'd ever seen before. It was as if they thought you were going to Africa on a safari. As soon as you walked in, you saw things like silk scarves printed with tiger's heads and high-powered rifles and ivory carvings of elephants. But the fifth floor was like being in the North Woods. Two canoes were manned by store dummies in red shirts. A tent was set up on artificial grass.

"Is Dad going to live in a tent?" Joel wondered.

His mother drew a breath and thought about that. "No. No, he particularly mentioned old army barracks. You'll be sleeping on a cot, I suppose. Although he didn't say so—"

"Mom, look!"

Joel pointed to a dummy reclining in a mesh hammock strung between fake trees. He saw himself in place of the dummy, lying on his back, looking up into real trees, swinging lazily and eating.

"Mom! Could I have one of those?"

"To sleep in?"

"Sure! And to hang around in. Please!"

"Well. . . Let's get your sleeping bag and see."

Something about lying suspended above the floor made Joel know he had to have that hammock. Even if he had to spend his own money. But his mother hadn't said no. She was feeling bad about leaving him and was open to coaxing.

Sleeping bags weren't very exciting. Joel's only question was, would it fit in the hammock.

"Can you sleep in that hammock?" his mother asked.

9

"Oh, certainly," the salesman said. "But you'd need a down bag, then, a light-weight one." He showed them a dark green, puffy bag that could be stuffed into an unbelievably small carrying bag. He also fetched the hammock, rolled to softball size.

"You won't have trouble carrying those," his mother said. "Too bad your clothes won't roll up that small. I think while we're here, I'll get you a knapsack. Would you like that?"

"Wow, yes! The hammock, too?"

"I guess so. It seems quite a bargain. I have a hunch conditions out there are pretty primitive."

"What's primitive mean?"

"Simple. Uncivilized. No furniture, no electricity."

"No TV?"

"Not without electricity."

Joel's heart sank.

His mother read his mind. "Darling, you can get along without *Star Trek* for two months."

"I don't know," Joel said.

"You'll have your transistor. You can take comfort in that."

"Yes," Joel agreed politely. But once again he began to wonder. He was pretty sure he'd be miserable. After all, his father didn't even want him.

They chose a red knapsack, and he felt better again. Maybe it wouldn't be so bad. They were heading for the elevator with their packages when his mother stopped.

"Joel, come here a minute," she called. "How would you like a safari jacket like this? Look at all the pockets."

Joel studied the jacket. "Could you make one?"

"Oh, I think so. If I worked *very* hard," she teased. "I might even work up the design for my spring collection," she added thoughtfully. "Your father can't say you aren't well dressed. That reminds me, it'll be just after Father's Day when you get there. It would be nice if you took him a gift."

They looked in the fishing department, but he didn't fish. And he didn't hunt. And he didn't smoke. And he didn't often wear neckties. At last Joel saw a display of knives.

"Mom! Maybe he'd like a knife."

They leaned over the counter. "Maybe he would."

Joel chose one and paid for it with his own money. Gift-wrapped, the present looked impressive.

"That was fun," Joel said as they left the store with all their packages. "Maybe it'll be all right out there. What a crazy name, though—Great Rat."

His mother nodded. "It sounds as if it must have been overrun by rats once."

"Maybe it still is! Great big rats."

"Mercy!" his mother said.

In one of the sci-fi magazines there was a story about a whole planet inhabited by rats, a whole civilization. Joel felt particularly glad he had the hammock.

"I'm going to put these things away," his mother told him, "until you're ready to go."

That was okay with Joel. He still didn't want to think about the summer any more than he had to.

11

2

D.J.

One day Joel's mother told him his father had phoned, on a rare trip to Long Island and made the final arrangements. Joel went to his room and ate a candy bar.

Another day his mother had drawn a sketch of the safari jacket. She asked if he liked it. In her drawing the boy wearing it looked slim. Almost skinny. Joel could see he'd be of more use to his mother if he wasn't so fat. The clothes she made him would look like the ones she drew. While she searched through her racks of cloth for suitable material, Joel fingered the dressmaker's forms. One, a boy of about Joel's age, was a lot smaller around the middle. Joel sighed.

In the next days his mother made a pattern for the jacket, cut the pieces, and stitched them together. When he tried it on, it fit all right, but his stomach pooched out. He felt fat.

Then, suddenly school was ending. Kids were talking about vacation and camp. Even the teacher asked about his plans. He said gruffly he was going to visit his father,

and felt grateful that she didn't ask any more.

His mother had finished the safari jacket. His other clothes were clean and ready to go into knapsack or suitcase. They lay on the bottom bunk, along with his hammock, the Father's Day present, and his sleeping bag. His mother was packing her own things to take to Europe.

And then it was the evening before leaving. His mother was waiting when he came home from walking the neighbor's dog. "How would you like to eat in Chinatown?" she asked.

He felt pleased; that was his favorite dining-out food. They walked, because Chinatown was nearby.

While they were eating, his mother explained how he was to get to Great Rat Island. "I'll take you to Penn Station," she said, "and put you on the train. I'll ask the conductor to make sure you get off at Sag Harbor. He'll keep an eye on you. There'll be taxis at the station, and you'll tell the driver to take you to the marina. That's where the boats tie up. Do you want me to write all this down?"

Joel said yes, hoping she'd stop talking about it, but she didn't.

"You'll have to tip the taxi driver," she said, "but you can do that. You had decimals and percents in school last year."

Joel made up his mind he would tip a quarter, whatever the fare came to. He didn't trust himself to do figures in his head while travelling.

"At the marina you'll have to ask for Captain Bell's boat. He'll expect you. He takes supplies to the island every week, your father says. Once you get on board, you'll be all set."

To Joel's embarrassment, his eyes suddenly filled. "I wish I didn't have to go!" The words seemed wrenched from him.

"Oh, darling, *don't!* You'll make me cry, too! The waiter'll think we don't like his food," his mother said, between a sob and a chuckle. "I know you're scared, but you'll like it; I promise you will."

"How do you know?"

"I just know. Look, I'll even admit I might be wrong. What if I send a letter with you, telling your father that if you're absolutely miserable, he's to send you back to Grandma and Grandpa? Would that make you feel better?"

Joel nodded.

When they left the restaurant, his mother surprised him by saying, "Come on, let's buy Chinese pastries to take home for dessert." She bought two of every kind Joel chose from the glass case. "It won't hurt this once," she joked. "You won't get any Chinese pastries on Rat Island."

There were more pastries than they could eat that night, so they finished them early the next morning, before she took him to the train.

Everything happened the way it was supposed to. Joel was resigned to his fate and went along quietly. He and his mother carried his knapsack and suitcase downstairs. A taxi came along, and they took it. At the station they found their way through cavernous walkways down deeper and deeper stairs to where the trains lay panting in the darkness.

The lights were on in the train they entered. His mother settled him in a seat, put his baggage beside him, and went outside to talk to the conductor. The conductor looked at him through the window and turned away. Joel's mother came back inside. They were early, almost the only ones in the car.

She kissed him. "I'm going now, Joel." Her lips trembled, but she smiled. "I'll write," she promised. "It'll reach you sooner or later. The letter for your father is in your suitcase." She gave a brief wave and fled. Through the window he saw her go up the steps.

She was gone. And so was the conductor. How did his mother know the conductor hadn't looked in and then forgotten all about him? He felt in his pocket for the directions. Luckily the paper was still there. People began coming on the train in greater numbers then. He wished they'd start so he'd have something to look at, something to take his mind off the worry.

At last the car did begin to move. And at the same time the conductor began collecting tickets. It was the same man, and he did seem to remember.

The train came out of its tunnel and apartment buildings gave way to houses. At first more people kept getting on, but as strips of open country began to separate the towns, people got off. Then the conductor had time to talk, and he stopped by Joel's seat.

"So you're going to Sag Harbor. Going sailing?"

"My father's camping on an island," Joel told him.

"Which one?"

"Great Rat."

The conductor nodded thoughtfully. "Isn't that a bird sanctuary?"

"Yes, I guess so. My father's an ornithologist."

"*Is* he? Well, sounds like you'll have a good summer." He moved off down the aisle.

Joel began to feel a little better. He found himself looking forward to the boat ride.

When the conductor came through again, he was calling, "Sag Harbor, last stop!" He paused beside Joel. "Can you handle all that?"

"Yes." Joel took his suitcase in one hand and the knapsack in the other. The sleeping bag was fastened to the knapsack.

"Don't get lost on that big island!" The conductor grinned and went on to the next car.

Joel decided he was joking. The island was probably very small.

As soon as Joel got off the train, a man said, "Taxi? Where you going?"

"To the marina—the boats."

"Right this way." He put Joel's baggage in the trunk of a cab.

There was another passenger in the taxi, a young woman. She had straight brown hair, brown eyes, and a safari jacket almost like Joel's. She smiled, and Joel smiled back, but neither of them spoke. Joel was glad when the driver got in and whisked them away. But there wasn't much to see out the window until they came in sight of the water and the boats, and then he couldn't look because he was busy getting his money out.

In the end paying was simple. The ride was seventy-five cents. Joel gave the man a dollar, so there wasn't even any worry about making change.

Luggage in hand, he decided to find a men's room. He didn't know how they managed such things on boats, or if they did. The one on the dock was at the back of a restaurant. When he came out, he had to ask several people before he found someone to direct him to Captain Bell, but he wasn't worried. Nobody seemed in a hurry. No boats were going out. It was still early morning.

The boats were nosed up or backed up to a long wooden walkway over the water. As Joel proceeded along it, a tanned and tough-looking man in a blue sweatshirt came to meet him.

"Hello, Slim! You Joel Curtis?"

Joel flinched. He'd as soon be called Fatty as Slim. That was what they meant, anyway.

"Yeah," Joel said.

"Captain Bell here. All set for the desert island?"

"I guess so."

"Need some help with that suitcase?"

"No, thanks," Joel said. He might be fat, but he wasn't weak.

They came to a boat that was bigger and more weather-beaten than most—it looked plainer, too, almost home-made—and Captain Bell turned into a narrow walk between it and its neighbor. From the walk he leaped

nimbly to the rocking deck, reached up for Joel's suitcase and knapsack, set them on the deck and offered Joel
a hand.

"Look out, now," he said.

Joel ignored the offered help and jumped. The deck
heaved, and he landed like a ton of lead, nearly losing his
balance. Straightening up, he looked around and saw
that the young woman was also on board. Joel stared at
her and she looked surprised, too.

Captain Bell said, "Well, the mist seems to be clear-
ing. I'll get up to the wheelhouse. There's coffee in the
galley, miss." He disappeared around the corner of the
cabin and then reappeared overhead in the glass-enclosed
part. They heard the engine start, the deck vibrated, and
the boat backed out of its mooring.

"Going to Great Rat Island?" the young woman
shouted above the noise.

"Yes. Are you?" Joel asked in astonishment. He had
thought, from the noises his father made over the phone,
that no women would be there.

"Yes, I am," she replied. "I'm replacing someone who
couldn't stand the loneliness."

Joel felt glad at that. He wouldn't be the only new-
comer. She wouldn't know her way around either.

"Have you ever been there before?" he asked.

"No, have you?"

"No. My father's there—Marshall Curtis. My mother's
gone to Europe. Do you know my father?"

"Only by reputation. He has a fine reputation as an
ornithologist. I'm lucky to have a chance to work with

him. My name's D.J. What's yours?"

"D.J.?" Joel screwed up his face in puzzlement.

"Diana Jo, really. But that doesn't sound serious enough for a scientist. Everyone calls me D.J."

"Mine's Joel," Joel said. He thought he knew what might have happened. "Does my father know you're a girl?"

She looked surprised. "I don't know! I don't think it matters," she added.

Joel thought it might matter. His father would be surprised at least, which made him feel better. Not only did he have company in his newness, but he suspected D.J. was also someone his father wouldn't be glad to see.

The boat was leaving the harbor and chugging out into open water. "Come on," D.J. said. "Let's go up front. Maybe we'll see some pelagic birds."

"What are those?"

"Birds that live mostly at sea."

She had binoculars around her neck. His father would like that, Joel thought.

3

Great Rat Island

At the front of the boat there was space to walk between the side and the cabin. Joel peeked inside, through the small windows. He made out two bunks covered by bright blankets.

Other boats sprinkled the water. "Commercial fishing boats," D.J. said. Land was still visible on either horizon, but it dropped behind as the *Bluebell* kept her course.

Joel would have asked more questions, but it was hard to talk above the noise of the engine. The wind blew the words away.

A small gray bird flew beside the boat, its feet almost touching the waves.

"Petrel!" D.J. shouted. "They never leave the ocean."

"Never?"

"Only to lay eggs. Then they nest on islands far out to sea."

Presently Joel saw land ahead. He pointed. "Is that it?"

"Too big, I think."

D.J. jumped up onto the roof of the cabin to ask the

captain. He was above them, looking out of his glass-enclosed wheelhouse. For the first time Joel noticed that D.J. was wearing sneakers. His father had given orders for him to wear his construction boots. Joel hoped D.J. had some boots in her suitcase.

She came back and sat casually on the low roof. Joel was impressed by how at home she was, as though she'd been on a boat many times.

"That's Owens Island up ahead," she told him. "It's belonged to the Owens family since before the Revolution. Before that it was a hangout for pirates. Blackbeard is supposed to have buried treasure there. Want to look at it?" She showed Joel how to focus the binoculars. Looking, he saw beaches and trees, and a meadow, but no houses.

"What do they use it for?" he asked, handing back the glasses.

"I guess they live on it. Summer homes, anyway. On the other side, maybe."

"Do we have far to go?" he shouted. It was only ten-thirty, but he was hungry.

She shrugged.

Owens Island fell behind on their right, and the ocean ahead appeared perfectly empty. Then they began again to see an island, straight ahead.

Captain Bell rapped on the window. D.J. and Joel looked up. The Captain pointed.

"He means that's Great Rat," D.J. said.

The island seemed low and very small at first, but its aspect changed and lengthened as they came nearer to its boulder-strewn shoreline. Joel stared as D.J. studied it through binoculars. It was to be their home for the next two months. There wasn't much to be seen—a rocky hill, barren except for some scrubby bushes, a gaping cement structure like a lookout, white birds flying above the boulders. Nobody seemed to be watching for the boat.

"The terns are here, at any rate," D.J. said.

Joel watched momentarily. They were dashing back and forth in the air, and now and then one would pause, spread its tail, and hover in one spot. But he was too eager to see his father to be interested in the birds. That could come later, maybe.

Captain Bell took the *Bluebell* in a neat arc around the end of a long wooden dock built over rock-strewn water. The hillside here had been cut back and faced with cement. Painted on the cement wall, in letters a foot high, was a sign:

BIRD SANCTUARY

DO NOT LAND WITHOUT PERMIT

INSTITUTE OF COASTAL SCIENCE

The terns wheeled and darted about the boat for a few minutes with excited cries, and then flew off about their business. Two men came bounding along a path at the foot of the hill.

Joel stared at them. Neither one was his father. He hoped he could remember what his father looked like. Yet he couldn't exactly call his face to mind.

The men came running out along the high, narrow

dock, and leaned against its rickety rail while Captain Bell put the boat alongside. Both were young. One man was black and bearded; the other very tanned and blond. Both wore tattered shirts, blue jeans and sneakers.

The blond man leaped to the deck and tossed some ropes to the other man, who tied them to posts. The boat edged closer, protected from scraping the dock by rubber tires hung over the side. Captain Bell cut the motor. The blond man stood braced against the pitch of the deck and looked questioningly at Joel and D.J.

"Hi," D.J. said. "I'm the new replacement."

"You are! Cripes, Marshall never told us we were getting a woman. Hey, Horace!" he shouted up at the other man. "She's the new student!" He grinned and stuck out his hand. "I'm Gary. That's Horace."

They shook hands, and he looked inquiringly at Joel. "Who're you?"

"Joel Curtis. Is my father here?" Joel looked hopefully toward the beach. No one else had come down the path.

"Marshall's kid? He told us you were coming *next* week!" Gary glanced helplessly at D.J. "He's not here. Went to Owens Island to look at ospreys' nests. Must've forgot the date. It's hard to keep track out here."

Captain Bell came down the ladder from the wheelhouse.

Gary said, "Howdy, Captain. Is this our stuff?" He indicated the cardboard cartons stacked near the after rail.

"Not only the cartons, but the young lady. *And* the young man. Can't say I didn't bring anything good this trip."

Gary said, "Captain, you deserve a drink! But Marshall keeps the good stuff locked up. Coming ashore?"

The captain looked at his watch. "No time. Got to go to Connecticut from here."

"Okay, next week, when Marshall's here." He turned to D.J. and Joel. "Is this all your gear?" He passed their things up to Horace, who lined them up on the dock. Horace put a hand down for Joel and heaved him up as though he weighed nothing. An instant later D.J. was standing alongside. Joel clutched the flimsy weathered rail firmly. Between the two warped planks under his feet he could see the water. But worse, the boat, heaving against the pilings, made the dock move, too.

The cartons were soon unloaded. Gary scrambled out onto the dock. Horace cast off the mooring lines, Captain Bell started the engine, and the *Bluebell* backed away.

Gary said, "There goes civilization. You got the mail, Horace?"

"Right here." Horace tapped a packet of letters slipped into one of the cartons.

It was impossible to move around much. D.J. was nearest the land.

"Go ahead," Gary directed. "We'll bring your stuff."

But D.J. slung her dufflebag over her shoulder, took her suitcase in the other hand, and picked her way to land like a cat. It was all Joel could do to carry his suitcase across the dizzying space. If you fell, you wouldn't even fall into water, but mostly onto rocks. He made it, but he didn't know how. Gary followed, carrying a carton and wearing Joel's knapsack. He didn't even look where to put his feet.

Horace and Gary preceded D.J. and Joel. The weed-lined path led uphill from the beach. On the way Gary dropped back to talk.

"We'll take these to the kitchen and then show you around. We can fetch the rest of the stuff later. Okay, Horace?"

"Sure."

"Boy, what a surprise! The old man's going to be surprised, too. I'll bet you can cook."

"I tend to burn things," D.J. said. "I expect you know what I mean?"

Joel wasn't sure he knew what she meant, but it must have been funny. He could see Horace's shoulders shaking, though Gary seemed disappointed.

"Who's been doing the cooking?" D.J. asked.

"We take turns."

"That seems like a good arrangement."

"Oh, it is, it is! I just thought maybe you liked to cook."

"He means he *hoped*," Horace said over his shoulder.

Gary grinned. "Okay, so I hoped. Nothing wrong with hoping."

The path led up between rocky hillsides covered with weeds, then curved sharply round one of the hills to a flat, open space. Here, the hillside appeared to have been cut away in one big bite. A square courtyard had been formed, surrounded on three sides by banked earth walls as high as buildings. In fact, set in the back earth wall was the brick front of a building, with two doors and four windows.

"That there's the lab and kitchen," Gary announced.

"How civilized!" D.J. exclaimed.

Joel didn't think it looked civilized. Weeds were growing right up to the doorsteps and on the hill above it where the roof should have been.

"What did you expect?" Gary asked.

"Oh, tents . . ."

"Didn't anybody tell you? This island used to be an artillery fort until guided missiles made guns obsolete. We think this building must have been headquarters. There's gun emplacements and cement pillboxes and underground storehouses. Not to mention underground passages! Really underground. This building, as you can see, is not underground but underhill.

Horace and Gary stomped through one of the open doorways and dropped the cartons of canned goods as though glad to be rid of the weight. Joel and D.J. followed inside and looked around. Joel saw two green camp stoves side by side, a long wooden table, and cans of food standing on open shelves.

"That's the lab in there." Gary pointed through an open doorway. "You'll see plenty of that later."

Horace was sorting the mail, laying it in three stacks on the table.

Gary said, "Let that stuff wait, Horace. You've got all week to read your girl friend's letters. Let's show them where to put their stuff." He said to D.J., "There's one wooden barracks still intact. When the army abandoned the island after World War II, the natives out here scavenged everything they could carry away. Including window frames. But the roof's practically water-proof. We keep pretty dry, except when it's windy and rainy."

D.J. said, "I gather we share the dorm?"

"Uh—yes, I guess we do. We weren't expecting a woman."

Joel felt cheered. He was going to put his bed next to D.J.'s, if possible. The thought was comforting.

Still wearing Joel's knapsack, Gary led them out of the weedy courtyard along another path to a weathered wooden building with a black roof.

"That's our tarpaper roof—see?" Gary explained. "It'll last the season, if you're lucky. Marshall wouldn't spend money for anything more permanent." He gave Joel a sharp glance. Joel pretended not to be listening.

From behind Horace suddenly said, "She can sleep in the corporal's room."

"There's no door," Gary objected. "Some privacy."

"Well, it's *more* private," Horace argued. "Door or no door."

"I'll take it, sight unseen," D.J. said.

Joel's heart sank.

But when they entered the building with its gaping window spaces facing the sea and the air wafting lazily through it, smelling of sun and weeds, it seemed a pleasant bedroom. The building was nothing but a board floor, wooden walls, and a slanting wooden roof. Six rusty metal cots were lined up in a row down the middle. Extra clothing hung on nails or lay on the floor.

"Not the neatest place," Gary apologized. "I hope you brought an air mattress."

"Yes. Is this the room?" D.J. started toward a doorway at the far end. Horace followed.

"How about you—what's your name? Joel?"

Joel shook his head.

"What did you bring? Just a sleeping bag?"

Joel nodded. "A hammock," he added.

"Hey, that sounds great! Where is it?"

"In the knapsack."

"Oh! Forgot I had it on." Gary shrugged out of the shoulder straps and dumped the bag on the nearest cot. Joel rooted around in it till he felt the ball of rolled-up mesh and pulled it out.

"Hey, that's great!" Gary repeated. "Have you slept in it?"

"No, but that's what it's for. In the store a dummy was sleeping in it."

"Where do you want to hang it? We've got hooks at the lab."

"Down there." Joel pointed to the end nearest D.J. She and Horace had begun moving a cot into her room.

"We don't have to stand here and watch them," Gary said. "We can carry in her gear." He picked up D.J.'s suitcase and indicated for Joel to bring her dufflebag.

Except for size, the small room was the same as the big room. D.J. began unpacking while the boys stood around talking about colleges. Joel hung out the window looking at the sea. The sun was shining, but a faraway haze hid the horizon.

Gary's school was in California, Horace's in New York City. D.J. was going to Cornell. Joel knew that college. His mother and father had met there.

D.J. spread her air mattress on her cot and unrolled her sleeping bag. "What do you do about washing clothes?" she asked.

Joel's mother had worried about that, too. "They must do something," she'd said. "You can't possibly take enough clothes to last two months."

Gary said the usual practice was to send a bagful of dirty clothes to town with Captain Bell. The laundry returned the clean clothes to the boat.

Everything around looked so clean Joel didn't see how he could get very dirty. Even the ground looked clean—light brown earth sprinkled with light gray rocks.

After D.J. was settled in, Gary consulted his watch. "I don't know about you guys, but I'm hungry. Let's eat. After lunch we'll give you a tour of the island while we check the traps." His glance included Joel. "Not but what you'll both have your fill of it after a week."

Joel wanted to explore the island, but he also wanted to see his father. What if his father came back while they were gone?

The island wasn't very wide, but it was long. The water he looked down at from the dormitory was on the opposite side from the dock. The building where the kitchen was must be about in the middle.

"When's my father coming back?" he asked.

"He didn't say." Gary laughed. "Whenever the caretaker gets tired of craning his neck at osprey nests and brings him back, I guess. There's no point in waiting for him. He told us to show you the work."

"Sure," D.J. said. "I want to see what you're doing.

I'd just like to meet Curtis and get it over."

Joel understood how she felt. He wondered if his father would like the Father's Day present. When the others started back to the lab-kitchen place, he lagged behind to take the box from his suitcase and the letter his mother had written and put them both in his pocket. Then he ran down the path after the others, his hands free of suitcases, almost belonging on the island already.

At the entrance to the courtyard Gary halted. "Hey, Horace, was the bread in your load?"

Horace shook his head. "My load was too heavy, man, to be anything but cans."

"We better bring the rest of the stuff up," Gary said. "There'll be hell to pay if Marshall finds it there."

"Is he hard to work with?" D.J. asked.

Gary said, "We don't know how he is with women."

They made Joel feel funny, as though they were talking about some stranger. But then he felt Horace's hand on his shoulder, and Horace's deep voice said, "Let's say he has more rapport with birds than with people."

D.J. nodded wisely.

Gary looked at Joel, then said, "Come on," and plunged off down the path to the dock.

They think I don't know what they mean, Joel said to himself. But I do. It means Dad likes birds better than people. Mom told me that.

4

A Program of Work

They ate salami sandwiches with mustard. Nobody noticed how much Joel ate; they all ate a lot.

"We get up before daybreak," Gary said. "Around five o'clock. By nine thirty at night we're ready to turn in. Anyhow, there's nothing to do after dark. You can't read because the lantern draws insects. We've already listed *them*. Part of the island's ecology, you know."

When they had eaten an orange apiece, Horace added their knives and cups to some other unwashed dishes. "We wash up after dinner," he explained.

From the kitchen they went into the laboratory and talked about scientific things, which Joel decided didn't concern him very much. He thought he'd like to go back to the dock and watch for his father. He was easing out the door when Gary called him.

"You better listen, too. Your father's going to expect you to know what's happening here."

So Joel stood around. He even listened for a while. Gary showed him and D.J. strings of aluminum bird bands in different colors, like bead necklaces. One size was for baby terns and another for adults. Joel's father had worked out a code that told things about the bird by the combination of bands on it. The parent birds were trapped when they came to the nest to feed their chicks. The scientists brought them to the lab and weighed them by sliding them headfirst into a paper cone that fitted on a scale. Then the birds were banded and turned loose.

"Doesn't it scare them?" Joel asked.

"Maybe," Gary admitted, "but they have short memories."

"We *think* they have short memories," Horace amended.

D.J. was interested in the records, and the talk moved off in other directions. So Joel sat on a stool and watched out the window for his father. Then he pretended he was at a space outpost. The expedition had crash-landed. . .

He returned to earth at the sound of his name. Gary was looking at him.

"What?"

"I said, if your old man agrees, I'm going to teach you to run the boat. I got this boat to follow the terns when they fly out to fish," he explained to D.J., "but I can't watch birds and look where I'm going at the same time. You can swim, can't you?" he asked Joel.

Joel shook his head. He was afraid of the water. Anyhow, this was supposed to be his vacation.

"Swimming's our chief entertainment here," Gary told D.J.

Well, it wasn't going to be his, Joel thought. However, he decided he might as well listen. Maybe his father really would expect him to know. All three students were writing a thesis, something like a theme. Gary was studying the terns' feeding habits. He'd bought the boat so he could visit the waters they fished. Dead birds found on the island were brought in so Gary could examine the contents of their crops and gizzards.

Horace was interested in mutations. He kept records on chicks born with abnormalities.

"Let's give them the grand tour," Gary said. "We'll see the boat coming in time to get back. I suppose you know—the birds fight intruders." He took a hat like a pith helmet from a row of similar ones hanging near the door. The hat had a ragged hole in the top about the size of a quarter.

"Don't tell me they made that!" D.J. exclaimed.

Gary nodded. "Well, not all at once. Repeated attacks."

"That's what you get for shoving them upside down into paper cones," D.J. said, laughing.

Joel eyed the hat suspiciously. "What's that white stuff?"

"Droppings," Gary admitted. "Only they don't just drop. They aim."

Joel noticed the boys' shirts were dotted with white splotches, too.

Gary plopped the hat onto Joel's head. "You get used to it," he said.

"After all, it's only rotten, digested fish," Horace added.

D.J. laughed.

Joel said, "Ugh!" but nobody paid attention.

D.J. chose a hat. She didn't seem to mind the idea of getting dumped on. The boys donned their hats, and everyone trooped outside.

"The island's long and narrow," Gary began explaining. "It's impossible to tell how much the hills were moved around by the army engineers. The granite around the shore was brought from some New York City subway excavation to keep the shoreline from washing away. That's why we have only the small beach near the dock. Horace, you got the chick-banding stuff?"

"Sure thing." Horace touched the string of beads dangling from his shirt collar.

Field work, Joel understood, consisted of trapping and banding as many birds as possible. D.J. would take over her share as soon as they showed her the procedure. She would check certain areas every morning for new nests and hatching chicks.

Gary said, "We do the chick check before the sun gets hot, so when the birds are chased off their nests, the eggs or hatchlings aren't exposed to the heat. Actually, the weather's been good. A lot of foggy days, but not much rain."

"I'd like to see some chicks hatch," D.J. said. "Wouldn't you, Joel?"

Joel nodded. It was the first thing he thought he would like.

"You'll see plenty," Gary promised, "starting tomorrow morning."

They set out along a gravelly path that Gary said had

been a road. Joel bounded ahead.

"Hey, stop!" Gary shouted. "You'll step on the nests."

Joel stopped too late. Something crunched underfoot. He couldn't see anything in the long grass, but his shoe was bright with egg yolk. For one awful moment he thought: They'll tell my father! I haven't even seen him, and already I'm in trouble.

Gary stooped and began searching the grass. He said mildly, "That's what happens when you don't look where you're going."

Joel began to hope. Perhaps what he'd done wasn't unforgivable. But a broken egg was so final. As in the rhyme, "all the king's horses and all the king's men" couldn't put it together again.

"I thought they nested in beach-type areas," D.J. protested.

"The common terns do," Horace said. "These are roseate terns. Roseates hide their nests."

"Here it is." Gary parted the grass tufts. "One egg left. See, here's what they look like." He pointed to an egg a little smaller than a hen's. "Common terns' eggs look the same, but more splotchy. You'll soon learn to tell them apart." He stood up. "Got this nest?" he asked Horace. "This is Horace's territory," he explained.

Horace pulled out a wooden paddle like an ice cream stick, with a number written on it. He laid the paddle beside the nest and wrote the number on his clip board.

Gary turned to Joel, who was surreptitiously wiping his shoe against his pant leg. "You'll learn to spot nests in the open. But stay behind me for now."

So Joel took his place in line. He felt Horace's hand on his shoulder in a reassuring squeeze. "Ask Gary some time how many he broke," Horace murmured.

Joel drew a deep breath. Maybe it wouldn't be too bad here if Horace and D.J. were his friends.

They came to another wall, like a dam, built from hillside to hillside across the little valley where the path ran. This wall was gray cement. The only opening in it was a doorway, leading to darkness.

"We call this the Mayan Temple," Gary said. "Because that's what it reminded us of. One of the main nesting areas is up there." He pointed to the top. Marshall goes that way at sun-up." Gary showed them a steep path. "But we won't disturb the birds now. We'll go through the storehouse. Take my hand," he told D.J. "Joel, take her other hand. If we fall in a hole, Horace'll pull us out."

The sun was very bright, but as soon as they stepped through the door, the dark overwhelmed any reflected light. Joel stumbled along, holding D.J.'s hand tightly. Their footsteps echoed. Joel began to feel frightened, despite D.J.'s firm grasp. But she began to giggle.

"Where are you taking us?" she demanded.

"Just to the stairway. It's not a trick, honest. Here, feel . . . That's the door jamb. Now the first step . . ."

"Got it," she said, then, "Joel, feel the stair?"

"Yes," he gasped with relief.

"Okay, there's a turn here. I don't mean a bird!" Gary announced.

Joel began to see D.J.'s outline ahead. Above her Gary stood faintly illuminated in a corner of the stairs. Joel rounded the corner behind D.J. and ascended into daylight. He found himself in a cement-walled room. Three walls had long slit openings near the top. The slits were curtained with burlap, but on one side the burlap was pulled back.

"The terns!" D.J. exclaimed as Gary and Horace joined them. "What a great lookout!"

"Where?" Joel cried, jumping up. The slits were too high for him to see anything but sky.

Horace brought a tall stool from one corner. "Here—climb up on this."

The ground outside was level with the lower edge of the opening. More than a hundred terns were arriving, departing, or just sitting, facing seaward. When one tern arrived, it took the place of another. They were sitting on eggs! Something small and furry moved beneath one tern. A downy brown chick!

Gary told them the weedless area was the roof of the underground storehouse. The terns liked the disintegrating cement as well as a beach.

Joel carried the stool to the other side and held the burlap aside. From there he could see a lot of ocean. Weeds marched down the hillside to the rocks below. And not far away was another, smaller island.

"That's Little Rat," Horace said behind him. "Want to look?"

"What's on it?"

"An old, falling-down cement building, on the other side."

Joel adjusted Horace's binoculars the way D.J. had taught him and stared across the sparkling water. A deserted island. For the first time he began to feel as though he were taking part in an adventure.

Going back through the underground storehouse wasn't bad. They could see sunlight flooding through the doorway.

Then, as they strolled along the path, the boys questioned D.J. about her project. She was studying bird migration. She explained to Joel that scientists still don't know how birds keep from getting lost when they fly south and return.

"I've brought mist nets," she told the boys. "I have permission to band migrating warblers."

"How long are you staying?" Horace asked.

"As long as the project holds out. Aren't you?"

"One more month, and we're through!" Gary exclaimed. "We've already been here two."

Horace grinned. "Don't mistake our lack of enthusiasm for lack of enthusiasm."

Gary said, "I never want to see another egg! A new face, though, does make life brighter. With all deference to your old man, kid, he's not the life of the party."

Joel kicked a stone.

"Cool it," Horace told Gary. "You wanted parties, you should've stayed in California."

"True," Gary grumbled.

They passed the barracks and climbed a rough stairway that led uphill from the courtyard. From the top Joel could see the water on both sides of the island.

"From the depths to the heights," Gary said.

"Hey, you want to see an underground railroad?" Horace slid down a steep path to where rusty tracks lay hidden by weeds. The tracks led around a curve to a cement-lined opening in the hill they'd just been standing on. Joel stared into the darkness.

"What was this?" D.J. asked.

"We think the army had a little donkey engine to haul stuff. The tracks go through another storehouse and out the other end to the emplacement for the big gun.

They climbed out of the cutting, back up to the ridge and followed it to the end. There they looked down on a cement pit full of water. "That was where the sixteen-inch gun sat," Gary said.

He next led them along the edge of another breeding ground to the lookout Joel had seen from the boat. Terns hovered screaming, they dived at the human invaders. Joel was on the verge of being terrified.

D.J. threw an arm around his shoulders and pulled him close. "Scary, isn't it?" she said. "You'll get used to it in a minute."

Joel stood stiff with fear, but she urged him along the path.

"See," she said. "They don't really attack. They know we're bigger than they are."

The birds wheeled away with angry cries, as though warning them not to come back.

The lookout, when they reached it, had about the same view as the other one. Stairs led down to the railroad storehouse. But there was no time to explore because Horace spied the boat coming from Owens Island and they had to start back.

The way they took back led past the tern traps, and Joel understood why Gary and Horace were wearing denim bags stuffed under their belts. Five adult terns were gently taken from their nests under the five traps and placed in the bags. They stayed quiet in the dark until they could be weighed and banded.

"We can do more trapping now that we'll have your help," Gary told D.J. "We like to tend the traps every hour."

When they arrived at the lab, Gary hung the bags on a row of nails. "These birds'll be all right for a few minutes," he said, and they hurried down to the dock.

Joel had left his father's present on the kitchen table. He wondered if he should run back and get it, but he felt timid about going by himself. Not that the island was exactly wild, but . . . He thought of the diving terns and decided to stay where he was.

He needn't have worried about recognizing his father. The thin, bearded man in suntans who leaped from the boat was the figure he remembered. Marshall Curtis waved to the departing motorboat and strode along the narrow planking. Binoculars around his neck were as much a remembered part of him as his beard.

Joel sprang to his feet and ran down the rocky shore. "Hi, Dad!"

His father stared. "Joel? By gosh!"

Joel rushed to hug him. His father returned the hug with one arm, holding his binoculars aside.

"I thought you weren't due till next week," his father said.

"No, this week!"

"I must've lost track. Well, you're here, anyway. Have a good trip?"

"Okay."

Marshall Curtis started up the incline to where the others waited. Joel grabbed his hand and pranced beside him. Now they would see that this really was his father.

"Do I see a woman?" Marshall Curtis exclaimed under his breath.

Joel said, "That's D.J. She came on the boat, too."

"Don't tell me that's the graduate student!"

"I think so."

"Another female Cornellian!" his father muttered. Joel sensed that the less his father was reminded of his mother, the better.

D.J. was introduced. Marshall Curtis said discouragingly, "I hope they warned you that things are primitive here."

"They did," D.J. said. "Professor Smith also said it was worth putting up with anything to work with you."

Marshall Curtis grunted and started up the path. Joel walked beside his father, still holding his hand, but he glanced over his shoulder. Gary and Horace were laughing.

Marshall Curtis said to D.J., on his other side, "Well, you're here. I suppose we'll have to make the best of it."

"Thanks," D.J. said.

Joel peeked around his father. D.J. was looking straight ahead, and she was mad. Joel was glad he wasn't a girl; his father never would have let him come.

In the kitchen Joel presented the Father's Day gift. His father seemed to like it. He asked Joel about school and then sat down to read his mail. The boys and D.J. were in the lab, banding the terns they'd brought in. So Joel was left wondering what to do with himself. He went outside and sat on the long bench, until finally Gary came out. He took Joel to the bunkhouse, as he called it, to hang his hammock. When they returned to the kitchen, Marshall was telling D.J. more about the tern study, and other things he was doing or hoped to do.

It was Gary's turn to cook. While he did that, Joel's father made out a new work schedule. Joel sat and watched him. His father's hair was thinner than Joel remembered, and his beard had gray hairs in it. His face was lean. Joel couldn't see any resemblance to his own round face. His father's eyes were blue. Joel's mother was fond of saying Joel looked like her family—dark-haired, dark-eyed. He loved his mother, but he wished she wouldn't say that.

His father looked up. "What's the matter?"

"Nothing," Joel said.

"You haven't seen me in a long time, is that it?"

Joel shrugged. That *was* it, but he couldn't say so.

"You'll be sick of the sight of me by the time summer's over," Marshall predicted. "Ask Gary."

"I'm sick of the sight of you now," Gary said. "Thank Heaven for D.J."

Marshall ignored Gary's kidding. "How are you at washing dishes, son?" he asked.

Joel couldn't believe his ears. "No good," he muttered.

"You'll improve with practice," his father said. "I'm putting you down for dishwashing duty. I'll help tonight so you'll know how we do it."

Joel didn't know whether to be glad for tonight or dismayed for the future.

"Gary says he wants to teach you to run the outboard," his father continued. "I don't think you'll have any trouble."

Joel slipped outside before his father could think of more jobs, and Horace came out of the lab and sat on the bench beside him.

"Your father get you all organized?" he asked.

"Yes."

Horace laughed. "He does like to put everybody to work. But the days out here would go awfully slow if you didn't have something to do."

So after dinner Joel learned how the dishes were washed. It was getting dark by the time they hung up the dishpan. Gary lit a lantern and led the way to the bunkhouse.

Joel's father smiled when he saw Joel's hammock and said he hoped Joel wouldn't fall out of it. D.J. helped Joel find his pajamas before she took the lantern into her room. The men undressed in the dark. Once in bed, Joel wasn't frightened at all because he could hear the others breathing or turning over, and his hammock was cozy. Outside the night was blue, not black.

5

Some Eggs
Are Missing

It was still dark when Joel heard the others getting up. He had discovered he could wiggle about, provided the edges of the hammock stayed taut. It was like sleeping in an oriole's nest. He had been planning to stay in bed, but his father shook the hammock.

"Joel."

Joel grumbled sleepily.

His father jiggled the hammock again. Thinking he was being tipped out, Joel started up with a cry.

"Get dressed," his father ordered. "I'm going to teach you to help with the chick check." He waited until Joel slid out of the sleeping bag and put his feet on the floor.

The gray light showed Marshall fully dressed. Horace was sitting up rubbing his beard. Gary was pulling on his pants.

"See you at the lab in five minutes," his father said and strode out the door.

Joel pulled on his clothes.

"Hey, D.J., you up?" Gary called. "The boss gave us five minutes."

A muffled answer came from the next room.

Joel was still half-asleep when he followed his father to the top of the Mayan Temple. They walked right into the nesting area, and the next moment he was wide awake and rigid with fear.

The birds rose in a screaming, flapping mob. Joel recoiled. He'd have plunged back down the path but for his father's shout: "Stay behind me and watch where you step."

The terns wheeled and dived like fighter planes. Their beaks looked hard and sharp. None of the outraged birds actually struck at the human intruders moving among their precious eggs, but their racket was so intimidating Joel could think of nothing but their anger. How long was his father going to keep him here?

Something splattered on his pith helmet. Not raindrops: excrement.

He was following so close that when his father stopped, Joel bumped into him. Despite the pale light, his father evidently had no trouble spotting nests. "Here's a new one." He grabbed Joel's arm and pointed at the ground.

At first Joel could see nothing but broken cement and twigs. As he stared, however, a spotted egg took shape.

"That's a nest?" Joel shouted above the raucous cries. It was like no nest he'd ever seen.

His father nodded. As Horace had done, he laid a

numbered stick beside the nest and wrote on the clip-board. "All the nests get numbers," he shouted in Joel's ear. "We keep track of each egg as it's laid."

Joel's hope that they wouldn't stay long had to be abandoned. His father went from place to place, distinguishing nests from cement and weeds with seeming ease. Most already had numbered sticks beside them. Then, like a magician, from the bare ground his father plucked a fluffy chick.

"Give me your hand," he told Joel. He laid the chick in Joel's left palm. Its little deep orange legs stuck out between his fingers. The soft webbed feet folded like leaves. The little creature barely struggled, but Joel could feel its strongly beating heart.

"Now take this . . ." Joel's father slipped a tiny blue band onto a funnel-like strip of aluminum. "Lay it over his leg, and pull out the aluminum. Gently . . ." The aluminum banding tool removed, the blue band closed loosely around the delicate ankle. One bright baby eye looked up at Joel.

"Nine nine five," his father said, writing the number. "Okay. Put it back in the nest."

Joel laid it back in the spot his father had taken it from. Marshall Curtis took up an egg and held it to Joel's ear.

"Hear anything?"

Something was ticking like an erratic watch.

"Starting to work its way out," his father said. "But never try to help. It has to free itself." He laid the egg back on the ground and moved away.

Joel followed, looking back at chick 995. Leaving it exposed on that rocky surface seemed wrong. What if it rained? He tried to look skyward, but an irate bird swooped at him, perhaps the chick's father. The parents would probably return to the nest as soon as *his* father stopped disturbing them.

He trailed around while his father banded more chicks, but chick 955 still seemed special.

They finished the Mayan Temple area and moved on. The birds behind them settled down. But overhead a new flock screamed and threatened. It went on and on, until Joel and his father had covered his entire share of the island. By the time they returned to the kitchen, Joel was so hungry oatmeal with powdered skim milk tasted good.

"I banded a baby tern," he confided to D.J.

"So did I," she said. "Aren't they sweet?"

"You ready to learn to run a motorboat?" Gary asked after breakfast.

"I can't swim," Joel said.

"I'll get you a life jacket. Why don't you come, too," he urged D.J. "Once you start to work with the mist nets, you'll be busy whenever the weather's nice."

They waited outside while Gary disappeared into a cement cave behind the lab. He came back lugging a green outboard motor.

"It's small," he apologized to D.J. "But it's okay when the water's calm. Here, Joel . . . see if this fits." He motioned for Joel to take a faded orange thing from atop the motor.

49

Joel put his arms through the holes, and D.J. tied the strings in front. Glancing down, he decided it made him look ridiculous—fatter than ever. He tore at the strings, wanting to get it off, but Gary said, "Hey! Leave it on!" So he followed Gary and D.J. down the path like a walking balloon.

The aluminum rowboat was pulled up on the small beach. D.J. and Gary launched it, then Gary waded out to attach the motor. He said, "I never know whether to leave it with the boat or not. Somebody coming by could take it. I usually bring it in."

D.J. sat in the prow. Joel had to wade out over slippery rocks before he could climb into the middle, facing Gary. Ha! Joel thought, and his mother had been so sure he was going to spend a safe summer here.

Gary said, "Here's how you start it, or try to." He showed Joel how to pull a string until the motor racketed to life.

"Okay, this is the way you steer, so simple a child could do it. You want to go left, you push this handle to the right. You want to go right, push it left."

After they were away from the island, he made Joel sit beside him. Turning over the handle, which he called the tiller, to Joel, he said "Okay, Joel, let's go that way."

Joel pushed the tiller in the opposite direction. The boat obligingly turned the way Gary pointed.

"Okay, now steer the other way."

Joel did so.

"That's all there is to it," Gary said. He moved to the middle seat, to balance the boat, leaving Joel alone with the motor. He and D.J. both had binoculars. They began sweeping the water for birds. Joel looked back. The island was still there. It looked too big to lose. But just the same . . .

"Let's see you take us over that way," Gary said. "Put the tiller over easy."

Joel turned the boat. For a while it was fun, but D.J. and Gary soon became absorbed in searching for birds and talking about birds. With no one to talk to himself, Joel decided that sitting surrounded by empty water and empty sky wasn't very exciting. The island was nothing more than a gray lump on the horizon.

"Where we going?" he called to Gary. But Gary had spotted some bird. The sun felt hot, despite the wind. Joel's stomach gave him a pinching request for food. He didn't like being out here, and there was no way to get away. Unless, of course, he steered the boat homeward. Gary and D.J. kept their binoculars to their eyes or searched the sky. Would they pay attention if he turned back?

They were almost back before Gary noticed. "What did you do?" he shouted. "Steer in a circle?"

D.J. laughed. "You forgot to set a course, Captain. Anyhow, this kid's getting sunburned. You should have worn your pith helmet," she told Joel.

He remembered his mother had packed a great tube of sunburn cream and admonished him to use it.

Marshall was typing at the kitchen table when they walked in. "Did you teach Joel to run the boat?" he asked.

"Too well," Gary said. "He got tired and steered us back home."

"It's just as well," D.J. said quickly. "I want to get started on my project."

"Come on," Gary said, "I'll help you put up the net." They left.

Joel felt his father looking at him. "It was dumb," Joel said. "And hot. There wasn't anything to do but sit there."

"You were doing a job," his father said.

"Well, it wasn't any fun."

"We're not here to have fun. I let you come because I thought you might be of some use. So don't expect to sit around eating and reading comic books."

"I don't read comic books!"

"Whatever they are—science fiction. You're not with your mother now. You're here to work. I want you to go out to the barracks and put on some suntan oil, and then come back and help Horace get lunch."

Joel stumbled out. The bright sunshine made his eyes water. His face burned. Sunburn. He was right to come back! And his father . . . He was too angry to think about his father. But one thing he did know: his father *was* having fun. He liked what he was doing.

D.J. was in the barracks, smearing herself with oil. She made sure Joel covered his neck and arms as well as his face, and once again he felt glad she was there.

"Living with a bunch of men takes getting used to," she said. "They act tough to impress each other. How would you like me to teach you to swim?"

Joel shook his head.

"Did you bring a swimsuit?"

He admitted he had, but he didn't in the least want to learn to swim.

Everyone, it seemed, went swimming in the evening before supper, so Joel had, perforce, to put on his bathing suit and go along. He waded in the shallows, pretending to hunt for scientific things. D.J. swam for a while and then called to him. He pretended not to hear, but his father said, "Go on son. This is a good chance to learn. You're not a coward, are you?"

Joel thought he probably was, but he didn't want his father to know. He pictured himself drowned. His mother would have something to say if that happened! She would be so mad! It would be worth it, almost. Fatalistically he waded to where D.J. waited.

After several days of this, instead of drowning, he discovered he had learned to swim a little. He could go from one barnacle-covered post of the dock to the next, even when the water was over his head. D.J. had been right, the water wasn't so scary once you got used to it.

In the meantime, his father had decided that Joel would be best employed in the morning getting breakfast while the others made the chick check. So while they tried to cover every foot of the island, labeling nests and banding newly hatched chicks, Joel cooked oatmeal with raisins in a double boiler, made coffee, and measured and mixed Tang and powdered milk. After he got through the worry of the first couple of times, it became rather fun. Especially since D.J. and the boys made it clear that they appreciated not having to wait for coffee when they came in. Joel hoped his father did, too, although he never seemed to care what or when he ate.

During his free time Joel explored the island, and even, with his flashlight, the underground vaults. He spent two long, boring afternoons with Gary in the boat, sitting patiently with a sci-fi paperback while Gary tried to obtain samples of the fish the terns were catching.

Sometimes he helped D.J. with the mist net. She only put it up during sunny daylight hours because the birds caught in it struggled and lost the oil from their feathers. If that were to happen on a foggy day, their feathers would get damp, and the birds would be chilled and die. It was called a mist net because, when stretched, its fine black threads looked like nothing more than mist. Birds tried to fly through it and were caught. The terns quickly learned to avoid it, but D.J. caught sandpipers and song sparrows and redwing blackbirds. When the warblers started migrating in August, D.J. explained to Joel, she hoped to catch and band them.

Joel didn't feel so good about doing dishes every night, but sometimes Horace or D.J. helped, and sometimes they all sat around the table, talking and joking. It really wasn't too bad.

One morning the *Bluebell* arrived, and Joel realized he had been there a week! With the mail was a letter and a postcard for Joel from Paris. The postcard was of the Eiffel Tower. His father said "Hmmf!" Whatever that meant. When Joel wrote his mother, he told her he was learning to swim and having a pretty good time.

He should have known it wouldn't last.

Next morning at breakfast his father said, "I found eggs missing at the Mayan Temple. Did anyone else?"

Horace, Gary and D.J. shook their heads.

"Are you sure?" Gary dared to ask.

"Certainly I'm sure. It's in my records."

"What could have happened?" Horace asked, puzzled.

"Maybe something took them." Joel thought he was making a good suggestion.

"Of course something took them!" his father exclaimed. "The question is what."

"Rats?" D.J. risked Marshall's scorn by asking.

"There are no rats here," Marshall said. "Leastwise we haven't seen any. A gull or a night heron may steal an egg from an outlying nest, but not this wholesale disappearance . . . and all from one area." He scowled at his coffee. Then, inevitably, his eye fell on Joel.

"Do you know anything about this?"

"No!"

"You haven't been running around up there?"

"No."

His father shook his head. "I don't understand it," he told the others. "Maybe I'll have Joel keep watch for a few days. If it's a rat, we'll soon know."

6

Vicky

As soon as breakfast was over, Marshall Curtis handed Joel his old beat-up binoculars and strode off down the path.

Joel hurried to catch up. "Where are we going?"

"To the blind. I want you to stay there till we find out what's going on."

"What do I have to do?" Joel asked.

"Keep an eye out," his father said.

"Just sit there? All day?"

They were passing the barracks. His father paused. "Maybe you'd better get something to read. But be quick. I'll wait here."

In the empty barracks Joel dived at the books under Gary's bed. He picked one with a lurid cover, the kind his mother didn't like him to read. It just fit his jacket pocket. He rejoined his father carrying a sci-fi magazine and the transistor.

At the underground storehouse his father paused. "You've been through here, haven't you?"

Joel said he had.

"Follow me, then." His father plunged in as though he could see in the dark. Joel made a snatch at his father's coattail before blackness swallowed them both. He kept his hold until they reached the stairs.

In the lookout his father set the stool close to an opening. "Sit here and try to keep one eye on what's going on out there," he said.

"What if I get thirsty?" Joel asked.

"After lunch you can bring a canteen. I'll send someone to call you to eat."

Joel, listening to his father's footsteps descending the stairs, felt a moment of panic. The only way out was through the dark. No, he could climb through the lookout openings. To do so would mean running the gauntlet of screaming birds, but at least he wasn't trapped. He looked at his watch. Eight o'clock! And he was supposed to spend all day staring at birds? This was the craziest thing he'd ever heard of.

Outside terns were flying to and fro, brooding eggs, courting, squabbling. Halfgrown chicks were begging for fish or trying to steal fish. On the roof overhead more terns talked in low, growling voices.

Joel sighed and took a comprehensive look at his surroundings. The post overlooked the tip of the island, a great deal of empty sea, and the near side of Little Rat Island. With binoculars Joel scanned the horizon. Not an enemy ship in sight. Great Rat became an island on . . . Where? The planet Pluto. He was the lone survivor of a spaceship, and hiding. The inhabitants appeared to be birds, but weren't. They had a language. If he could learn to speak it . . .

He gazed at Little Rat. As on Great Rat, boulders lined the shore. Beyond them grew pine trees, dense enough to hide anything—a cave, a castle, a buried treasure. Gary's boat could get him there to find out. The idea appealed to him. He thought he saw something moving among the trees. Horace said the island was empty, but a bear might be stranded there. Or a chimpanzee, escaped from a zoo. Imagine finding a tame chimpanzee!

Outside where the terns sat, the heat began to rise in waves. Inside, warm air hovered motionless. The morning was endless. Joel grew drowsy.

Before he knew it, Gary was shaking him. "So this is how you watch!" Gary exclaimed.

Joel's heart sank. He'd been careless. "Don't tell my father," he begged.

"I'll see," Gary said ominously. "Let's hope no more eggs are gone." At any rate, at lunchtime, he didn't mention Joel's napping.

During the afternoon Joel told himself that nothing could have happened while he slept. If the terns had been disturbed, their cries would have awakened him. I *would* have to get caught napping, he thought. But he was lucky, too. Gary hadn't noticed the book.

The following morning when Marshall came to the kitchen, Gary asked, "Any more missing eggs?"

"Not today."

"That's good." Gary gave Joel a meaningful look. "Is

it possible you recorded them wrong?"

"Possible," Marshall admitted. "However, I'll keep Joel out there a few more days. Keeps him out of mischief." He looked at Joel with the suggestion of a smile.

Joel felt pleased with himself. "If anything's taking them, I'll find out," he promised. "But what if it's at night?"

"We eliminate first one possibility and then another," his father said. "That's the scientific way of working."

Joel was making a sandwich to take to the blind when he thought of coffee. Grown-ups drank it to keep awake, why shouldn't he? He poured what was left from breakfast into a battered thermos he found on the shelf. At the barracks he picked up his transistor, Gary's book, and his flashlight. The dark storehouse was still scary, even though he knew the way. He wouldn't like to go without the light.

In the blind he looked over the nearest pair of nesting birds. His father had banded them with different colored bands, so that through binoculars the male and female could be told apart. The female was on the nest. The male flew down with an inch-long mackerel. One chick shoved the other aside and gobbled the tidbit. Joel hoped both were getting enough to eat. He'd watched the terns long enough to see how wasteful Nature was. Eggs got crushed, nests were abandoned, chicks died of exposure or starvation. It seemed wasteful until you understood that ants and other insects nibbled away at the waste, and herring gulls swooped in and grabbed.

The radio programs when he tried them sounded foolish and far away. The book wasn't very good, either. He took a look at Little Rat through the binoculars. Scrubby pine trees and granite. The same as yesterday. He went back to his book.

The terns saw the girl first. They took startled flight, throwing a patchwork of light and shadow across his page. Alerted, he looked out and then stared.

She was coming up the hill, threading her way among rocks and weeds—a kid a little older than himself, wearing cut-off blue jeans and a gray sweatshirt. Visitors! Was she coming to look for him? She couldn't be! They'd never send anyone to disturb the terns.

She came right on into the nests, and before he could shout, she picked something from the ground and put it in the orange bucket she carried. She was taking the eggs!

The terns were all in the air now, shrieking and screaming, almost as though they welcomed a break in the monotony. The girl was wearing a blue cap with a visor and was holding a broom handle above her head. The terns attacked the top of the broom handle and didn't come near her head at all. While Joel was noticing this, she picked up another egg.

"Hey!" he shouted. "Stop that!" His voice went unheard beneath the clamor, so he had to climb from the stool and lie flat in order to slide through the narrow opening. He rolled out onto the cement, causing, if possible, more commotion from the frantic birds.

He wasn't as brave about facing them as the girl was, but he had to protect them. The racket they were making would bring someone to investigate. He mustn't be found sitting by. He shielded his head with his arms and rose to his knees.

The girl stopped as though he, and not the birds, frightened her. Then she whirled and started back down the hill, going as fast as she dared with a bucket of eggs.

Joel jumped to his feet and ran after her.

"You can't have those!" he shouted.

She turned. "Who says?" she called up at him. Her hair under the blue cap was blond and straight. She looked like a friendly sort of girl.

"*I* say," Joel told her. "They belong to my father."

"They're not *his* eggs!" She set off again.

Joel hurried to catch up, crying, "Wait! Yes, they are! He's a scientist."

He ran headlong down the hillside and reached the path in time to cut her off. She was taller, but he was driven by fright. What would his father say?

"Give me those eggs," he demanded, blocking the path.

"Why should I?"

"It's stealing. They belong to the birds. And it's getting me in trouble." He made a grab for the bucket.

She held it away. "Don't be so mean! They won't miss a few! They've got hundreds."

"My father has them all counted," Joel insisted. "And I'll get in trouble."

"Really counted?"

"Yes!"

She looked down at the bucket for a moment. "Oh, all

right." She put it in his hands.

Possessed of the eggs, Joel had time for questions. "How'd you get here?" he asked.

"By boat, naturally."

"Who'd you come with?"

"Myself."

"All by yourself?" he repeated. "To get eggs? Why?"

"I was hungry."

Hunger always awoke Joel's sympathy. He thought of his sandwich. He could give her that. "Would you like a salami sandwich?" he offered. "And coffee?"

"Yeah, that's okay."

He hesitated, not wanting to run the gauntlet of the terns, yet not wanting to go through the storehouse either, without the flashlight. The flashlight was in the blind with the sandwich.

"Do you want to put these back?" she asked, indicating the eggs. "I know where I got them, but I don't know which eggs."

Joel wasn't going to worry about fine points. He carried the eggs while the girl held up her pole, giving the terns something to attack. She pointed out the nests she had robbed, and Joel carefully restored the eggs.

"What if a mother tern just laid an egg, and tomorrow it hatches?" The girl giggled. "Boy, will she be surprised!"

Joel's father would be surprised, too. Joel hoped it wouldn't happen.

They slid awkwardly into the blind. The birds settled down.

The girl looked around the room. "I like this. Are you camping here?"

"No," Joel said. "I was watching the eggs. Did you take some before?"

"When before?"

"Two days ago."

"It was early morning!" she exclaimed. "Nobody saw me."

"I told you—he has them counted."

"I'm sorry," she said. "I thought they'd be good to eat."

Joel was reminded of the sandwich. He gave it to her, and they shared coffee from the thermos cup, making faces as they drank it. The girl munched on the sandwich.

Her eye fell on the binoculars. She picked them up. "These yours?"

"Not exactly."

She put them back on the sill. "You've got to be camping here because there aren't any houses."

"There are buildings. We live in those. Me, my father, and three college students."

"I suppose you're the big scientist, and your father does what you tell him."

"Sure," Joel said, but he felt uncomfortable even joking about such a thing.

"What's your name?"

"Joel Joseph Curtis. What's yours?"

"Vicky Marie Owens. Victoria, really. Did you ever hear of Owens Island?"

"Where the treasure is?" Joel asked. "We passed it coming here."

"My father owns it," Vicky said. "He and my grand-

father and my uncles. Your father doesn't own this island."

"So what?" Joel said. "The birds own it."

"They do not," Vicky contradicted. "It belongs to the
Institute. I know that. Where do you live in the winter?"

"New York," Joel said. Like most New Yorkers, the
city *was* New York. The state of New York was . . .
well, upstate.

"I live in Connecticut in the winter," Vicky admitted,
"but I like it better here. Don't you?"

"Not really," Joel said. "My father doesn't like having
me with him."

"You live with your mother? Me, too. Where is she
now?"

"Paris. Where's yours?"

"Mexico, I think. That's what they said."

"Who?"

"My mother and stepfather. Do you have a stepfather?"

"No."

"No stepmother, either?"

"No."

"You're lucky. Why doesn't your father like you?"

Joel shrugged. "How come you have to eat birds'
eggs?" he asked curiously.

"I don't *have* to," she said. "I just thought it would be
fun. Like explorers, you know."

"What do they taste like?"

She pushed her cap to the back of her head. "Like
eggs."

"Chickens' eggs?" Joel had a terrible desire to taste one.

65

"Sure, like chickens' eggs. I didn't eat *all* of them," she added. "Some already had baby terns inside."

Joel made gagging sounds. Vicky laughed.

"Hey, can I look through the binoculars?" she asked.

"Sure."

She turned them on Little Rat Island. "It looks close through these," she remarked, and then, lowering them, "Hey! Who's that?" She pointed down the hill.

"Gary," Joel said. "I wonder what he's doing."

He was on the path that edged the rocks and he kept looking up at the hillside. While they watched, he left the path and started uphill.

"Will he come here?" Vicky sounded startled. She considered the dark stairway. "Maybe I could hide down there."

"What for?"

"Won't he be mad if he finds out I took the eggs?"

"He might."

"I'm not supposed to *be* here, even. The sign by the dock says No Trespassing. I know that."

"It's all right if you're visiting somebody. Like me."

She giggled.

"He's not supposed to walk around out there!" Joel said disapprovingly.

"He's coming right this way!" Vicky hissed. "Maybe he found my boat. How can I get away?"

"Down those stairs, if you don't mind the dark. It's a tunnel. Wait . . ." He handed her the flashlight.

"I'll leave it at the other end. 'Bye!" She started down the steps.

"Will you come back?" he called before she reached the turn.

She paused. "Maybe. How'll I find you?"

"Nobody comes here once my father's done his check. Usually." Joel glanced over his shoulder. The terns were in the air now. Gary would have to come right up and kneel before he could see in. "I'll come here every morning at eight," Joel offered. Vicky had a watch. "When might you come?"

"I don't know. My plans are very indefinite." She disappeared round the corner. Despite the noise of the birds, Joel thought he could hear her going down the stairs. He stepped away from the door, prepared to confront Gary.

Would she come back?

7

Visitors From Owens Island

"So you're awake." Gary's face peered in at the opening.

"How come you're walking around?" Joel countered.

"I'm not. I'm coming in." Gary slid feet first through the window, landing upright on the floor.

"Have you seen anybody?" he demanded.

Joel shook his head. It seemed less like lying.

Gary was breathing hard. "We've got visitors," he said. "I saw a boat. I wish I could catch them! That's what happened to the eggs. Bunch of vandals! If you see them, cut through the tunnel and find me. I'm going over to the west shore." He ran lightly down the stairs.

Joel realized he, too, would have to go through the dark, if he wanted lunch. Going out wasn't bad, though. At the bottom of the stairs you could see the rectangle of sunlight at the other end. All you had to do was cross the cement floor. His flashlight had proved the floor was level—no drains to fall into.

He looked at his watch. Only ten o'clock.

Gary reported the boat at lunchtime.

Marshall Curtis said, "I wish you'd stayed with it, instead of rushing around the island."

"I thought it was important to protect the terns," Gary said with dignity. "I'd have looked pretty stupid standing by the boat while people were taking eggs."

"You didn't see anyone, Joel?" his father asked.

Again Joel shook his head. He didn't have to tell, he reasoned. Vicky wouldn't take any more eggs. His father didn't have to know the details.

"Vandals may be the answer," Marshall was saying. "Given the times, I suppose it's inevitable. However, I wish you'd keep watch another day or two, Joel. Let's make sure it's not some critter. A rat or weasel on this island could do more damage than people."

After lunch Joel selected another of Gary's books, but the afternoon dragged nevertheless. The mystery was solved; he could expect neither an animal nor vandals. What did vandals look like, anyhow? he wondered. Tough boys?

The following morning was warm and sunny. Joel sat in the blind and thought of things he wanted to ask Vicky: What was it like, chugging around Long Island Sound alone? Wasn't she afraid? What if a storm came up? What was it like to live on Owens Island? Did they spend much time digging for treasure? Whose would it be—finder's keepers? Joel rather thought even treasure was taxed nowadays. His father had been to Owens Island. Did Vicky know him? Did she know where the ospreys' nests were? He wondered if he dared ask his father about the island. He pictured it with holes all over. and piles of dirt, but that probably wasn't right; they'd fill up the holes.

After supper that evening he hurried the dishwashing. He wanted to get out and see if he could find a place to hide Vicky's boat before it grew dark. That is, if she really wanted to visit him secretly.

Following the hillside path, he saw once again that the sides of the island were fairly steep. Anyone could look right down on a boat tied among the rocks. At the tip, however, the possibilities were better. Extra boulders had been piled there, and two flattish ones, standing on edge, formed a wall. Joel stood atop a rock and studied the possibilities. If Vicky's boat was the size of Gary's, she could hide it behind those two rocks. Even if the back stuck out, it might not be noticeable, unless the boat was bright colored. Anyway, he'd suggest it, if she came again.

He returned by the little-used path on the other shore, but found no better hiding place. By the time he climbed through the weeds to the barracks, it was dark. The others would be coming in soon, so he undressed, meaning to lie in his hammock and listen to the waves, but the sounds lulled him to sleep.

The weather next morning was unpromising. Joel got up when the alarm clock went off to find the barracks afloat in a world of gray. Wisps of fog drifted in the windows like lost clouds. By the time he dressed and stumbled outside, the fog had turned to drizzle.

Horace prophesied that it would clear up by afternoon —too late to expect Vicky.

It turned out that his father didn't expect him to keep watch in the rain. Joel protested that he was willing. (Vicky *might* come.)

But his father said, "Nothing's more miserable than a blind in the rain. I wouldn't ask it of anybody; I can barely ask it of myself."

"Have you?" Joel asked in astonishment. "Where?"

"More times than I like to remember. Did you think this business is all glamour?"

"You mean it's not all paradise islands like this one?" Gary teased.

"Gary should've been an oceanographer," Horace said. "There's glamour."

"I may yet," Gary said. "Especially if I flunk here."

Marshall looked amused. Joel was fascinated. He secretly admired Gary. It would be nice to make cracks like that, that made his father smile.

The weather didn't clear; the drizzle remained. They all spent the day in the kitchen and lab, reading, mending, writing letters and reports. In the afternoon D.J. showed Joel how a cake mix works. When the cake was done, everyone sat around eating it. Joel had to eat fast to get his share.

When Joel saw the sun next morning, he thought Vicky would surely come. But the long morning crept by, and she didn't. He returned to the kitchen at lunchtime with the sting of disappointment, and with nothing to look forward to until tomorrow. How could he possibly get through the long afternoon at the blind? And even if he wasn't at the blind, what could he do? He could swim almost around the dock, but that was no good without a friend to swim with. The trouble with this place was there weren't any other kids.

He hung around the kitchen after lunch, half-deciding to tell his father about Vicky so he wouldn't have to go back to the lookout. But Horace and his father were working together. If Joel told, he wanted to tell his father alone.

Gary was going out in the boat, having coaxed D.J. to take turns steering. Joel moved slowly in the direction of his duty, looking wistfully after D.J. and Gary. Going with them would be exciting compared to an afternoon in the blind.

Along the path the weeds called sweet clover grew higher than his head. Yellow butterflies danced above them. Joel stood and watched their aimless fluttering, and lingering there he heard voices.

Visitors! Gary and D.J. were coming back with three teenagers and a man in a yachting cap. Joel decided to join them. Surely his father wouldn't expect him to sit in the blind while there was company.

He met them where the path turned toward the kitchen.

"Hey, here's Joel," Gary said. "Professor Curtis's son," he told the newcomers. "Joel, this is Mr. Owens and some of his family."

Mr. Owens put his arm around the tallest boy. "My son, Todd," he said, "and my niece Kristin, my nephew Barney." They had a family resemblance—all tall and skinny. Kristin and Barney had braces on their teeth and shoulder-length hair the color of Vicky's.

Joel said, "Hi," and tagged into the kitchen.

Gary introduced Joel's father.

"I hope you don't object to visitors, Professor Curtis," Mr. Owens said.

"Certainly not neighbors," Marshall told him. "Your caretaker has been good enough to show me your osprey nests."

"These kids have been wanting to come over," Mr. Owens explained. "And I've been curious myself."

So Marshall Curtis talked about the tern project and D.J.'s plans to band migrating birds. The adults and Todd drank warm beer. Todd was starting college in the fall.

D.J. took Kristin and Barney off to one of the blinds. They invited Joel, but he'd spent enough time in a blind lately; he wanted to hear about Owens Island. Besides, he wondered why Vicky hadn't come. Was this man her father, or one of her uncles? She hadn't mentioned any brother.

When they were leaving, he got a chance to ask. Barney and Kristin had come back, very friendly with D.J.—as though they know her better than I do, Joel thought jealously.

Mr. Owens stood up. "Very interesting. But we won't take any more of your time. Did you kids find out all you wanted to know?"

Barney and Kristin said enthusiastically that they had.

"Thanks for the hospitality," Mr. Owens said. "We'll come by again, if we may. Next time we'll invite you for drinks."

Everyone walked them down to the dock.

When Joel saw the boat, he understood what Mr. Owens meant about drinks. The boat was as big as the *Bluebell*. It had curtains at the windows, and canvas chairs on the deck under an awning.

"Our island's supposed to have wild turkeys, too," Mr. Owens said. "I haven't seen any lately."

"I have," Barney said. Kristin said she had, too.

Joel sidled up to them. "What's Vicky doing?" he asked.

"Oh, do you know her?" Kristin said.

Joel nodded.

"She had to go to camp this summer," Barney said. "Her father's going to Italy, so she had to go to camp."

"I bet she hates it," Kristin said.

Puzzled, Joel watched them go. Did they mean Vicky was supposed to be in camp now? Wasn't she on Owens Island? And if she wasn't, when she left the other day, where had she gone?

8

Vicky's Secret

Before the alarm went off next morning, Joel was awake in his hammock, thinking. Vicky was supposed to be in camp! She hadn't actually said she'd come from Owens Island. He tried to remember. She had said her father and uncles and grandfather owned the island. But if she hadn't come from there, then where had she come from?

He understood why people said "dying of curiosity." He couldn't stand so many unanswered questions!

"What are your plans?" his father asked at breakfast.

"You said you wanted me to spend more time at the lookout!" Joel exclaimed.

"I don't want to be too hard on you. The *Bluebell*'s due this morning. Maybe you'd rather hang around and help unload."

"No," Joel said quickly. "No, I don't mind. Honest!"

His father said, "All right. I'd appreciate it if you'd make sure nothing extraordinary is happening up there.

No eggs are missing, but a couple of chicks have hatched ahead of schedule. I wonder if someone could have switched nest numbers."

"Who would do that?" Gary asked.

Joel's father shrugged. "It doesn't seem likely. Is it possible terns lay eggs in each other's nests?"

Joel gulped. So he and Vicky hadn't gotten the eggs back right. He gathered the dirty bowls, cups, and glasses, pretending he wasn't listening.

He wished they'd leave the kitchen so he could make two sandwiches—one for himself and one for Vicky, if she came. Finally they did leave and he put two quick sandwiches, a thermos of milk and the binoculars in his knapsack. He stopped at the barracks for his book and flashlight. Altogether he had quite a load.

In the lookout he dumped his knapsack and took up the binoculars. What if he really was on a desert island, and every day he had to hope for rescue? It sounded nice, but it was hard to imagine because the lookout faced the open Sound. Large tankers passed on the far side of Little Rat all week and on weekends the water was dotted with sails and motorboats. This morning, however, the sea was vacant.

He turned his glasses on Little Rat in time to see a small boat edging into sight around it. The sea was flat. The person in the boat looked—could it be Vicky? The sun glanced off shining blond hair. It *was* Vicky!

His heart beat faster. Should he run down to the shore? He took the field glasses from his eyes to see how far away she really was. If he went through the tunnel to avoid the tern colony, it would take a while to reach the shore. He raised the binoculars again. Yes, it was definitely Vicky, headed straight for the island. At last!

He ran down the stairs and through the dark echoing vault, hardly bothering to use the flashlight. By the time he circled over the hill and reached the point by way of the path, she was close in. He waved and climbed out onto the rocks. The tide was higher than when he had discovered the place, but the rocks still looked high enough to hide the boat. He signaled, and she understood. She brought the boat gently against the upstanding rocks and cut the motor. Her wooden boat was badly in need of paint, so its color certainly wouldn't attract attention.

"Hi!" Vicky shouted and tossed the rope to Joel. He almost caught it, and felt pleased to be allowed to tie it around a rock. Vicky climbed out to stand beside him.

Joel felt tongue-tied. He had so much to say.

"Hi," he said at last.

They made their way back to the path. Vicky looked toward the boat. "You picked a good place," she said. "I can't even see it."

"That Gary saw it last time," Joel told her. "That's why he was hunting you."

"Did you tell him?"

"No." Joel grinned. He sat on a rock. "They thought there was a boatload of vandals. My father bawled Gary out for not staying by the boat to catch them."

"Where's your father now?"

"They're waiting for the *Bluebell*. It comes this morning with the mail and food."

"I know. Are they still making you guard the terns?" Vicky laughed.

"Sort of. Not *making* me. I said I would—today. I was hoping you'd come," he added shyly. "There's something I want to ask you."

"Let's go up to the hideout," Vicky said. "I mean, lookout."

"Okay," Joel agreed. "I brought two sandwiches. And milk. Come on."

He led her around the point, over the hill and through the storehouse.

"It's *dark* going in," Vicky remarked, "even with the flashlight."

Joel let Vicky sit on the stool. Now that she had come at last, his questions didn't seem so important. Just having company was so nice.

"I looked for you every day," he told her. "Why didn't you come before?"

"I had things to do," she said vaguely.

"What things?"

"I had to go to town and get groceries one day."

"In that boat?"

"Sure."

"For everybody on your island?" he asked slyly. "Didn't anyone go with you?"

"No, just me."

"They don't even know you're there!" he announced.

Her eyes widened. After a pause she said, "How'd you find out?"

"They were here!" Joel told her triumphantly.

"Looking for me?"

"No," Joel admitted. "Visiting. A big boy named Todd, and his father, and Kristin and Barney. They said they're your cousins."

Vicky was sitting bolt upright. "Did you tell them about me?"

"No!"

"Then why'd they say they're my cousins?"

"I *asked* them about you. I asked where you were, and they said, in camp."

"What did you say?"

"Nothing."

Vicky was silent. "All right," she said at last, "I'll tell you. Promise you won't tell anybody? Even your father?"

Joel promised.

"The truth is, I ran away from camp."

"How?"

Vicky giggled. "The bus that brought us was taking other kids away, and all their junk. I got in the other line. They counted us when we got on. I thought I'd be caught, but the count was right! I guess some other kid got left." She laughed merrily.

Joel was impressed. "But how'd you get here?"

"I took the train back to New London, where I live. Then I went to the post office and bought a postcard. I wrote the camp that my mother had asked me to write because plans were changed and I was going to stay with my grandfather on Owens Island. They can't reach my mother, and if they telephone my grandfather, they'll be sorry. He's the crossest old man you ever saw! Especially when my grandmother's away. He's got arthritis. He doesn't approve of divorce, so he won't have anything to do with arrangements for us kids. Mean old beast! My grandmother has to be in the City this summer with my aunt. Otherwise, I could have stayed here, and my grandfather would've had to put up with me. I *love* my grandmother.

"Anyhow, I took the ferry to Orient Point. It was easy. And there I went to the yacht club. This man I know was taking out his sailboat to check the self-steering device before sailing for Bermuda. So he took me to Owens Island. I was going to see if I could stay at one of my uncle's."

"Where's your father?"

"I don't know exactly. He's supposed to go to Italy. Anyway, no one saw me arrive. The man let me off, and there I was. With all my camp stuff, clothes and sleeping bag. So I thought, why don't I just camp on an uninhabited island? So I did."

"How?"

"In that boat down there."

"You stole it?"

"No, I didn't steal it! It's my grandfather's—I suppose. There's a bunch of boats. Everyone uses them. They'll think somebody else has it. All the houses have docks."

"What did you do?"

"I put my stuff in it and filled up a gasoline can. Nobody saw me. But even if old Terence had seen me, he wouldn't have paid any attention. I've got so many cousins there! My uncles' wives' kids aren't even Owens, and they're there." She brooded over the injustice.

"Where did you go?" Joel recalled her to the story.

"I went to Little Rat."

"Little Rat! Right over there?" He pointed.

Vicky nodded.

"You've been living there?" It was the most exciting thing he'd ever heard.

She nodded again.

"How come I never saw you?"

"I stayed away from this side, naturally."

"Wow!" Joel said. "You stay there at night?" Aren't you scared?"

"No," Vicky said airily. "I wanted to be there at night, so I could study the stars. They wouldn't have let me do that at camp. Not late, like three in the morning. Stars move, you know. I'm going to be an astronomer."

"You mean—horoscopes?"

"No, silly, that's astrology. Astronomy is a science."

Joel's brow cleared. "You mean space travel!"

"Maybe. First I have to catch up with what they already know—like the constellations."

"The Big Dipper?"

"Everyone knows that."

Joel didn't know there were any others, but Vicky said, "I mean the harder ones—Libra, Sagittarius."

"What do you do if it rains?" He thought of the day before.

"You can't see any, natch," she said.

"Not stars!" Joel laughed. "I mean, how do you keep from getting wet?"

"There's a huge old cement building there. I can even bar the door. The army used to store things in it. Now it's abandoned."

"But you didn't have anything to eat except terns' eggs?" Joel began to think the adventure might not be so marvelous after all. Vicky set him straight.

"Of course I did!" she said. "The afternoon I got here I went back to town in my boat and bought drinking water and charcoal for a fire, and bread and cheese and canned stuff. And chocolate bars," she added. "They're good for survival."

Joel's mouth watered. He hadn't had a candy bar since he left the city.

"You must have money," he said, swallowing his lust for chocolate.

"I do," Vicky said. "Well, I had to have money to spend at camp, for horseback riding and crafts. My mother was feeling guilty. She gave me a hundred dollars."

"A hundred dollars!" Joel's mother had only felt guilty enough to buy him a hammock, and she was going clear to Paris, France.

Vicky nodded. "For two months. She knew I wouldn't throw it around."

Joel looked longingly toward Little Rat. "What's it like there?"

"It's fun."

"Could you take me some time?"

"Sure."

"What if somebody finds you there?"

Vicky shrugged. "I can bolt the door. For all they know, the building still belongs to the government. It says CAUTION all over the place

"What if they stole your boat?"

"I take the outboard off and keep it in the building," Vicky explained. "It doesn't weigh much."

"It's the same kind as Gary's." Joel felt glad to know something.

"So they can't get the boat away without any motor or oars," she said.

"They might tie it to their boat."

"If they do," she said philosophically, "I'll come out and tell them to stop. People don't steal boats out here. I bet I could leave it there a year."

"I'd stop on that island if I had a boat."

"No, you wouldn't. People in boats ride around. Or fish or something. Besides, look at all the empty islands there are . . ."

"Oh." Joel had supposed Little Rat was unique. When one thought of all the people in New York City, you would expect them to be sprinkled over the outlying islands, too.

"I chose Little Rat," Vicky explained, "because there's a big old tank there, full of rainwater. To wash in, you know."

"What do you do in the daytime?"

"Think. Fish. There was a fishing rod in the boat." She giggled. "I bet they miss that! But it was a kid's rod. The kid probably thinks he lost it."

"How long have you been there?"

Vicky counted on her fingers. "Six days, I think."

"How long are you going to stay?"

"I was thinking of staying all summer, but it's kind of lonesome."

Joel wished with all his heart he could join her.

"I was thinking of getting my dog," she said.

"Where is he?" Joel asked.

"At Owens Island. He's mine, but my grandparents keep him 'cause my stepfather's allergic. His name's Sirius."

"Are you serious?" Joel laughed heartily at his pun, but Vicky did not.

"That's the dog star, in case you don't know," she said.

"I've got some sci-fi magazines I could lend you," Joel offered.

Vicky turned up her nose. "That stuff's not real."

"It might be!"

"I suppose some of it's possible," Vicky admitted graciously. "Anyhow, you want to help me get my dog?"

"What could I do?"

"Run the boat, once I get him in it. I'll have to hold him, otherwise he jumps out."

Joel considered. "I can't get away," he said finally. "They'll miss me."

"They don't watch you every minute. You must be gone sometimes."

"Yeah, but if I don't show up for lunch, they'll notice I'm gone."

"It won't take us all day," she said. "We could go at night, actually."

"I have to go to bed. We all go to bed, right after dark."

Vicky saw the drawback in that. "What if we went early in the morning?" she asked after some thought. "About six o'clock. Nobody's up then at Owens Island."

"I have to cook breakfast," Joel objected. "I wouldn't have to stay and eat it, though. If I could think of some reason to leave."

"Can't you just leave?"

Just . . . leave . . . Joel thought deeply. It seemed a devil-may-care possibility. "I suppose I could," he said at last. "If I leave before my father comes in to breakfast. Except I'd probably meet him. He and Horace cover this end every morning."

"Hide someplace."

"Yeah, I could do that," Joel agreed.

"How long does it take them to look at all the nests?" Vicky asked.

"About an hour and a half," Joel said. "They finish around seven."

Vicky pondered. "What if I meet you where the boat is now about seven fifteen?"

Joel said, "Okay. If I can get away."

"If you're not there," Vicky told him, "I'll come back the next morning . . . if the weather's good. If it's foggy or rainy or windy, the whole thing's off, of course."

"I don't mind a little rain," Joel said.

"You can't go out in bad weather in a rowboat," Vicky said reprovingly. "Even with a motor. My father says that's suicide." She got up and moved to where she could look out at the sky. "I think I should go now. Today's a good day to go to town. I have to get dog food."

"Aren't you scared?" Joel asked. "All that way in that little boat?"

Vicky looked wise. "You know what they call Long Island Sound in the summer? The Dead Sea. That's from the Bible," she added.

Joel wished he could go with her. It seemed ages since he'd seen a town, a grocery store.

He went back to the boat with her and watched as she started the motor and put-putted away. Joel stood on the shore until the boat became indistinguishable on the glinting water. Back in the lookout he tried to find it with binoculars, but it was too far away. Boats chugged faster than one expected.

He stared at Little Rat. It had seemed so far away, but now here was Vicky, coming and going as if she owned it. Gary probably would've let him steer there, if he'd asked. Of course, he wouldn't have discovered a bear or a chimpanzee. It was Vicky's camp. And she was going to have her dog. *Serious,* what a dumb name!

The rest of the morning dragged. The afternoon was endless. But he had tomorrow to look forward to.

When he reported that nothing had disturbed the terns, his father said, "Thanks, son. One more day, and we'll call it quits."

"Maybe I'll start early," Joel said vaguely.

He didn't know whether his father heard him or not. He was already buried in one of the scientific journals that had come with the mail.

9

Joel Meets Sirius

Joel bounded out of his hammock the next morning with a sense of impending adventure. While he lit the kitchen stove and started oatmeal cooking, he wondered if Vicky, on her island, was getting ready.

He made two peanut butter and jelly sandwiches, wrapped them, and put one in each pocket of his safari jacket. He mixed extra powdered milk to fill the battered thermos, which he hid under his jacket. It was kind of sneaky, but he was having so much fun it didn't seem wrong—just secret.

As soon as the oatmeal was done, he ate a bowlful. D.J. and Gary came in as he was finishing, and Joel slipped out while they were eating.

He walked briskly to the barracks. The alarm clock there said six forty-five, half an hour to wait. He put the sandwiches and thermos in his knapsack, then sat on the end of Horace's bed, with one eye on the path and the other on the clock.

At five minutes to seven he saw his father coming from

the Mayan Temple. What if he came to the barracks!

Joel flew to the far side of the room, dropped his knapsack out of the window opening and let himself down after it. His jacket caught on a nail, but didn't tear much. He waited with beating heart for footsteps on the wooden floor. No sound came, so he made his way between the weeds and the side of the building to the front corner. No one was in sight. His father had gone to the kitchen as he was supposed to. Joel retrieved his knapsack and pushed through shoulder-high weeds to the shore path.

Behind the rocks, Vicky was waiting with the boat. Joel dropped his knapsack on the seat and jumped in enthusiastically. The boat rocked, and wood scraped granite.

"Hey!" Vicky yelled.

"I'm sorry." Joel sat carefully on the middle seat, facing her. He glanced at the hillside. "Let's get out of here."

She started the motor, backed away from the rocks, and headed into the sun.

"I brought sandwiches and milk," Joel shouted.

Vicky nodded. The motor and the splashing water made too much noise. Joel swung round to face the direction they were going. Crests of waves ran alongside. He had never been on the water this early. Fear clutched his stomach, and he turned to look back. Behind Vicky loomed the island. She gave him a conspiratorial grin, and he began to relax. She seemed to know exactly what she was doing.

He wondered if she could see the place she was heading for. In the clear morning air he could see a thin strip of gray like a pencil line on part of the southern horizon. That was Long Island. He took his compass from his pocket and offered it to Vicky. She grinned and shook her head, so he sat and studied it himself. According to the compass they were traveling southeast.

The next time Joel looked back, Rat Island had fallen far behind. He suddenly thought: What if I drowned? His father would never know what had become of him. If the boat sank, could he stay afloat? He wished he could talk to Vicky. In fact, he wished he hadn't come.

A petrel flew past, padding its feet in the waves like a child splashing through puddles.

He heard Vicky shout, and his heart thudded as he flung round to see what had happened. She was pointing ahead. He looked. Land had appeared as if by magic. Was that Owens Island? She was heading straight for it.

"Is that it?" he called.

Vicky nodded again, with a cheerful grin.

Soon he could make out a house at the eastern end. Vicky headed the boat toward a nearby line of sandy cliffs, topped by woods. A sandy beach ran at the foot. She chugged along this, outside the breakers. Then cliffs and woods dropped away, and knee-high grass covered a meadow, through which wound channels of water. Vicky ran the boat up one of the channels, turned off the motor and tilted it out of the water. The boat was still moving forward. She slid overboard into knee-deep water and nosed the boat onto a sandbar.

After the drone of the motor, the silence seemed deafening.

Vicky waded onto the spit of sand and stood, arms akimbo, taking deep breaths. She looked about with pleasure.

"I sure love this place," she said.

"This?" Joel looked about in surprise.

"Not this salt marsh, silly. The island."

How was he to know? He began to feel angry. Also hot. The sun shone relentlessly on the windless marsh. The grass sparkled like water. He took his jacket off.

"You can leave it," Vicky said in a more gracious tone. "We'll be back before the tide changes." She rolled her pant legs down. "Come on, we have to go this way." She set off through the grass. The house Joel had seen was hidden now by a line of trees.

Joel followed squeamishly. The grass roots looked as if water covered them when the tide came in. He felt as though his feet—or even more of him—might sink in, but the sand was solid. Vicky was marching confidently ahead. He thought about snakes, but the strange grass grew as separately as bristles on a toothbrush. There was no place for anything to lurk. He decided the marsh was safe enough and quickly caught up with Vicky.

Except for the building beyond the trees, Owens Island appeared uninhabited. Woods encircled the marsh. Inland beyond the trees rose a hillside meadow.

"Isn't it beautiful!" Vicky exclaimed. "When I grow up, I'm going to build a house of my own and live here the year around."

"How many houses are there?" Joel asked.

90

"My grandfather's . . . that's where we're going . . . Uncle George's, Uncle Earl's, my father's, my great-aunt's, her family's . . ." Vicky counted on her fingers. "Six big ones. Counting the caretaker's and the farmhouse and the guesthouses . . . twelve, maybe. They're on the other side, where the beach is. That's why I put in here." She looked at her watch and walked faster. "It's almost eight."

"How are you going to get him out?" In Joel's experience dogs lived indoors.

"Who—my grandfather?"

"No, silly, the dog!" Joel said, getting back at her.

Vicky took the snub good-humoredly. "I wondered why you wanted to get my grandfather out!" She laughed. "Sirius will be out. He has to sleep in the barn with the others. They're supposed to be watchdogs, but they aren't. They run around with the kids. Except Shep. Shep met me when Mr. Franklin let me off. And she didn't tell. Dear old thing!"

"Did you see your dog then?" Joel refused to call him by name.

"No."

"How do you know he's still here?"

Vicky stopped in her tracks. "He has to be!" She laughed. "He can't run away. And they can't give him away, because he's mine. My grandfather has Shep and her daughter Basket and Basket's puppy that Grandpa calls Fido, unless he's given him a better name. They're shepherds. Sirius is a cocker spaniel. He loves to swim. That's why someone has to hold him in the boat."

They entered the belt of trees.

"We have to be careful now," Vicky said. "Don't be scared if the dogs come running out. They know me. We'll coax them to come back to the boat with us. Then when we get to the boat, you can hold Sirius, and away we'll go!"

At the edge of the woods was a hedge, too tall to see over, but there were spaces at the bottom, little paths where dogs could slip through. Between the hedge and the house stretched a neatly clipped lawn. At the far side more hedges enclosed a rose garden. On the other side a row of white buildings ran down to the water. A white boat lay at the dock.

"What do we do now?" Joel asked, low-voiced.

"I'm not sure," Vicky admitted. "I thought the dogs would be outside. We'll have to spy out the situation."

They sat on the ground and watched the yard, waiting for something to happen. Joel wished he'd brought the sandwiches. An elderly shepherd dog strolled into sight around the house and lay down near the porch steps.

"There's Shep," Vicky whispered.

They heard footsteps in the house, and a man in blue coveralls came out the back door carrying a bucket. He set off toward the dock.

"That's Terence, the handyman," Vicky said.

Shep rose and followed him. Terence passed the barn and whistled. Two dogs very much like Shep bounded out.

"Basket and Fido!" Vicky exclaimed. "Where's Sirius?"

The three dogs followed the handyman to the dock. Basket and Fido leaped aboard the launch there. Shep crouched on the wooden walkway, seemingly content to see the adventurous ones off.

"Where is he?" Vicky cried, forgetting to keep her voice down. "Where's *my* dog?" She was kneeling in the sand, staring at Joel. He was shocked to see her blue eyes tear-filled.

"He'd have come out if he was here," she gasped. "What have they done to him?"

Joel offered the only explanation. "He must be in the house."

"He could be." Her face brightened.

Joel felt a sense of relief. Now they could give up this crazy business and go back to the boat. Because obviously if the dog was in the house, there wasn't any way they could get him.

But Joel had rejoiced too soon.

"There's only one thing to do," Vicky said resolutely. "You'll have to go in and find out."

"Me!" Joel stared at her, aghast. "Are you crazy? Why me?"

"I'll tell you why," Vicky said. "Because they know me, and I'm not supposed to be here. They'll just think you're somebody's kid. But nobody's going to see you. All you have to do is open the door, step inside, and call Sirius."

"There's someone in there," Joel objected. "I can hear her singing." Couldn't Vicky see how impossible her scheme was?

"She's in the *kitchen*. You won't have the least trouble, I promise. If somebody does see you, what could they do? Ask your name? So you say Joel Curtis. That's honest enough, isn't it?"

"Yes, but . . ." Joel knew he was being talked into something, and he wasn't sure he wanted to be.

"But what? Say you've come for the dog. Sirius loves children. If he's there—" Vicky's face crumpled.

"What if they want to know who I am?" Joel asked hastily.

"Say you're visiting." She nodded in the direction of the other houses. "Say you're visiting Kristin and Barney. You know them."

Joel sat up on his knees. How could he march into a strange house as if he owned it?

"Maybe the door's locked," he suggested.

"Nobody locks doors here," Vicky said. She folded her arms over her stomach as if she suddenly had a pain.

"What's the matter?" Joel asked.

"I can't stand not knowing what's happened to him," she said faintly.

"All right, I'll go." Joel got reluctantly to his feet. "Do I have to crawl through this like the dogs?"

Vicky unclasped one arm and pointed along the hedge. "Through there. Oh—I hope he'll be there!"

On the lawn Joel felt as though he were crossing a stage. I don't want to do this, he thought. Darn Vicky!

He trod lightly up the steps to the door and put his hand on the screen. It opened, and he stepped inside.

He found himself on a screened back porch, like his grandmother's in Staten Island, only bigger. The woman was rattling dishes in the kitchen, but he couldn't see her. He crossed the porch to a doorway and saw that a hall ran straight through the house to a big front door with glass. Sunlight was pouring through it. He wet his lips.

"Sirius!" he whispered. "Sirius . . ."

Two things happened at once: the telephone shrilled from its stand at the foot of the stairs; and a brown cocker spaniel came charging out of one of the front rooms, ears flying, furred feet slipping on the polished floor. The dog saw Joel, braced himself and began to bark furiously.

Joel stood his ground because he was afraid to run even though a man—Vicky's grandfather—stepped into the hall. "Sirius," he wheezed. "Cut it out!"

That was the dog who loved children!

The man gave the dog a shove with his slippered foot. Sirius barked harder. The phone added its clamor.

The man picked up the receiver and looked at Joel.

"Hold on," he growled at the phone. "What do you want?" he demanded of Joel.

Joel felt bereft of speech. Wordlessly he pointed to the dog.

"Get him out of here!" Vicky's grandfather shouted above the noise. "And next time—knock!"

Joel edged toward the porch. Sirius followed enthusiastically, barking without pause. He believed he was routing the intruder. Joel slipped outside and held the screen door open. Sirius stopped in the middle of the porch and put forth his best and loudest effort.

Grandpa Owens dropped the telephone receiver on the table and shuffled down the hall toward Joel. He put

95

one slippered foot beneath Sirius's tucked-up tail and booted him through the door. Sirius tumbled ignominiously down the steps.

"Don't be in a hurry to bring him back," Grandpa Owens said. "Worthless critter!" He removed the door from Joel's limp hand and closed it. Undeterred Sirius took up his stance on the grass and went on barking.

Joel heard Grandpa Owens shouting into the phone. "None of your business where Mrs. Owens is! No, ma'am, I will *not* give her a message."

A whistle came from the hedge. Sirius's ears went up; he stopped mid-bark and whirled. The whistle came again. Sirius became a brown silky streak racing over the crisp grass. Joel ran for the gap. He'd actually gotten the dog!

On the other side Vicky was rolling on her back, helpless with laughter. The dog made little dashes at her, cavorting, panting, wiggling his whole back end, pausing to lick her face before running in circles again.

She sat up when she saw Joel and tried to quiet Sirius, but he was too excited to stay still. Joel kept well away, not wanting to provoke him.

Vicky controlled her laughter long enough to say, "It's all right," and went off into another gale.

At that Joel began to see the funny side, too, though his knees felt weak. He dropped to the ground, and the dog came to sniff him, wagged briefly then ran back to Vicky.

"That's Joel," she said, hugging Sirius. "That's my good friend, Joel. He's your friend, too." She took a deep breath and jumped up, smothering her laughter. "Let's go!"

"Now we can talk out loud," she announced when they came out on the far side of the trees. "Oh!" She began to laugh again, holding her stomach. "I thought I would die when I heard him barking."

"I thought I would, too!" Joel began to laugh also. "You said he loves children!"

"I forgot how he barks at strangers," Vicky gasped. "What did my grandfather say? I saw him boot Sirius out the door. He always does that."

"He said he didn't care if I didn't bring him back."

"Well!" Vicky exclaimed. "It's a good thing we came and got him!"

Crossing the marsh they kept breaking into giggles. The grass and mud sparkled, seeming to laugh with them. A little breeze came up, ruffling their hair.

"Oh-oh," Vicky said. "It's going to be choppy going back."

While they tugged the boat off the mud flat, Sirius ran into the water.

"Now he's going to be all wet!" Vicky exclaimed disgustedly.

Sirius swam in a circle, holding his head up as though he feared to wet his chin. Finally he emerged to leap into the boat, where he shook himself, showering water all over Joel.

"Hold him," Vicky cried. She gave the boat a final push and jumped in.

Joel held Sirius by his collar, but Sirius sat quietly in the bottom, tongue lolling, happy to go anywhere with Vicky. She started the motor and they were off.

As they drew away from the island, Joel realized what she meant by choppy. The little waves seemed to chop at the boat, slapping the side and the prow and making the going rough. As sailors said, the wind had freshened.

Joel stole a look at Vicky.

"We should have a sailboat!" she shouted cheerfully, so apparently there was nothing to worry about.

Relaxed, Joel bethought him of the sandwiches and brought them out of his pocket. They ate and fed Sirius bits and passed the milk back and forth. By the time they finished, Great Rat was looming ahead. Joel felt marvelous. He'd really made the trip! And thanks to him alone, they'd gotten the dog.

Vicky brought the boat smartly in to the landing behind the rocks. Sirius would have leaped out if it hadn't been for Joel's hold on him.

Vicky reached for his collar. "Give him to me."

"How will you hold him and steer the boat?" Joel shouted.

"It's only a short way now. Maybe he'll realize he's in the middle of the Sound. Thanks! Thanks a lot."

Vicky's watch said eleven o'clock. Joel climbed out on the rocks. "When are you coming back?"

"I don't know. Soon. Watch for me. Mornings. Eight o'clock." She put the motor in reverse and the boat backed away. Sirius looked as if he was sorry to leave Joel behind, which was pretty funny, considering how he'd behaved at first.

As soon as Joel turned his back on the boat, he began to feel guilty for having sneaked off. Cautiously he made his way over the hill to the door of the Mayan Temple. He didn't have his flashlight, so he had to fumble through the dark. In the lookout nothing was changed. He stayed there, thinking about the morning's adventure, until the sun's position overhead announced noon.

In the kitchen nobody asked where he'd been. Everything was as usual. Joel began to feel pleased with himself. He and Vicky hadn't done anything wrong. But they had a terrific secret!

10

Weather Report

Joel spent two mornings at the lookout, but Vicky didn't appear. The second evening before supper he slipped into the lab. He was reading the titles of the books there when his father came up behind him.

"Looking for anything in particular?" Marshall Curtis asked.

"A book on stars," Joel said.

"Science fiction? You won't find it there."

"Not science fiction," Joel protested. "I meant constellations and stuff."

"Don't tell me you're getting a taste for reality?"

"I don't know what you mean." Joel stubbed his boot against the floor.

His father wouldn't explain. "Nothing, son. Wait a minute . . . *Natural History* has a diagram of the sky for this month. Let's look at that." He led the way to the shelf in the kitchen where he kept such useful items.

They opened the magazine on the table and studied it. The round diagram was black, with stars as pinpoints of white joined by dotted lines. The words looked impossible to pronounce. Joel felt helpless. If Vicky could figure those out, she was smart. But he did see one word he thought he recognized. Sirius. That was the dog's name. He was glad he had found that much.

"It looks complicated," his father said.

"What is?" Horace asked, coming in.

"Stargazing," Marshall said. "Know anything about it?"

"Star light, star bright, first star I see tonight," Horace quoted.

"The space program's looking for men like you!" D.J. exclaimed. She was taking her turn at cooking.

Joel laughed.

Marshall smiled. "Want to hold a seminar after supper, if it stays clear?" he asked. "Maybe if Horace puts his mind to it, he can work out this diagram."

"Sure thing," Horace said.

They took the magazine, a flashlight, and Joel's compass and climbed the hill across from the kitchen.

"This must be the only place on the island where no terns are nesting," Gary said as they scrambled uphill.

The waist-high weeds gave off a strong odor at night. The sky was deep, deep blue and moonless, but lights twinkled on the southern horizon. Some of them might be on Owens Island. The glow on the northern horizon came from Connecticut, over the curve of the earth.

The sky had many more stars than the map. Joel didn't see how the ancient Greeks could have imagined that a bunch of stars, with others sprinkled between, looked like a lion, or like Hercules. Only the Big Dipper made sense. He decided Vicky was showing off, pretending to study them. But he paid attention and tried to see what the others were looking at.

The magazine did tell things to look for. On certain nights Mars could be seen near the moon, on other nights Saturn or Jupiter. It said, "Saturn is near the crescent moon in the sky this morning." To see it, one would have to get up at four A.M. That might be what Vicky'd meant about being able to go out when she wanted to.

But clouds were coming up fast, blotting out the southern sky. Gary stood up on a rock, looking for points of interest on Earth, mainly lighthouses. Down at the water's edge Joel could see white bursts of waves against rocks.

Suddenly Gary said, "Hey! There's a light on Little Rat!" The others were trying to convince themselves they had located the constellation Virgo before the clouds covered it and paid no attention.

"There it is again!" Gary exclaimed.

Joel stood on tiptoe. "I don't see anything," he said finally. Did Vicky have a lantern? She probably did. She seemed to have everything she wanted. He must warn her to be careful, though tonight was the first time they hadn't all gone to bed soon after sundown.

"It's going to rain," Marshall Curtis said. "We'll try again. It takes practice."

"I wonder if somebody's camping over there," Gary said.

Marshall Curtis led the way downhill, with Gary still watching Little Rat. "It's gone now," he said finally and jumped down off his rock.

When his father was out of earshot, Joel said, "Gary, could I take your boat out alone sometime? Just around the island?"

"Don't you like my company?" Gary asked.

"Sure, but it would be fun alone." Joel thought of Vicky, going all over Long Island Sound, when all he wanted was to go to Little Rat. Surely he could do that much. "I'd wear the life jacket," he promised. "And I wouldn't go far."

Gary said, "Ask your father, but I'll bet he says no."

"It's your boat."

"But he's my boss, and your boss."

"He wouldn't have to know," Joel suggested.

"Hah!" Gary said with finality.

Joel had never seen his father so sociable. When Joel and Gary came into the barracks, D.J. was in her room, but his father and Horace were sitting on their beds, talking by candlelight. His father was telling how he'd watched night migrations through a telescope trained on the moon. You saw birds as they flew across the moon's face.

As Joel undressed, rain began pattering on the roof. He climbed into his hammock and slid into his sleeping bag. A lump there proved to be his transistor radio. He decided to turn it on, keep it close to his ear, and find some music.

Instead a voice came on, saying, *"If the hurricane maintains its present course and speed, it should reach the New York region tomorrow evening."*

"Joel!" His father's voice came across the room. "Turn that off!"

"There's a hurricane coming!" Joel protested.

"Nonsense!"

"There is!" Joel insisted.

"We can't do anything about it tonight. Turn it off!"

Joel did as he was told, but he wished he had the earplugs. What would the terns do if a storm came? What would the chicks do—the ones who couldn't fly? He wondered how the chick he'd banded, little 995, was getting along. The last time he'd seen it was when it left the nest. Chicks the age of 995 hid in the grass except when their parents brought food. His father would catch it before it could fly and give it an adult band. He'd like to know when his father rebanded it, but maybe it wouldn't live, if it got caught in a hurricane.

His next thought brought him sitting bolt upright. The hammock swayed, but he couldn't fall out as long as he kept the sides higher than his body. Vicky, alone on her island! He wasn't sure exactly what a hurricane did, but he knew it blew very hard, blew over houses and palm trees. A lot of water came, too. This island would be safe. Nothing could blow the kitchen and lab away because the building was bolstered by earthworks. But he wasn't sure how the building was put together on Little Rat. He wanted to ask about hurricanes, but the others were already asleep. Gary was snoring. It would have to wait till morning. Maybe Vicky would come in the morning, and he could warn her.

He thought of the hurricane as soon as he woke. He took the transistor to the kitchen and listened while he was getting breakfast.

Sure enough, a hurricane *was* coming! The radio announcer talked of nothing else. Gary, D.J., Horace, and Marshall straggled in eventually, served themselves, and listened.

"The storm is now moving northwest or northward, and is attended by a large area of hurricane winds and gales over an area five hundred miles in diameter. Extreme caution is advised for shipping in the Atlantic from Latitude thirty-two northward."

"Does that include here?" Joel asked.

"Sounds like it!" his father said. "You should have spoken up last night, Joel. I thought you meant Florida."

"We don't have those things in California," Gary remarked smugly.

"Big deal," D.J. said. "I suppose earthquakes are better!"

"Police have been advised by the weather bureau to be on the lookout for strong winds and high tides," the announcer said. *"Police emergency crews are standing by. Persons living in low lying areas along the coast should prepare for high tides. Stand by for further advice concerning this severe storm."* The announcer retired, and music came on.

"That'll put an end to this year's breeding season,"

Joel's father said with a sigh. "We can't expect the nesting
to survive that."

"What about us?" D.J. gave a shaky laugh.

"Yeah," Horace seconded. "When they say *high—how*
high?"

"We'll be all right in here," Marshall Curtis told them.
"This part of the island is high enough to escape the
waves, and you couldn't ask for better protection from
the wind than to be set in the hillside like this. We'd
better take what we want out of the barracks, though.
And move the beds in here. No point in sleeping on the
floor."

"Have you ever been in a hurricane, Marshall?" Gary
asked.

"The edge of one," Joel's father said. "In the Bahamas.
We were doing work on flamingos."

"The word 'hurricane' comes from the Caribbean
Indians," D.J. said learnedly. "The Mayan Indians, too.
They called the god Hunraken and threw a young girl into
one of their wells every year as a sacrifice so Hunraken
would bring rain."

"They threw in gold, too," Horace said.

"Yes," D.J. agreed. "Did you know that's where all
the Mayan museum pieces come from today? All the
gold the Spaniards wrested from the Indians they melted
down into gold bars, partly because they were horrified
by the Mayan religion. It *was* pretty horrible."

Before Joel could ask for details, Marshall Curtis said,
"I believe we can turn this weather to account."

Gary gave D.J. and Horace a long-suffering look.

"D.J.," Joel's father directed. "You and Joel pack your gear and then go out to the blinds. I want you to watch the terns. See if they sense a storm coming, take notes on how the fledglings behave, everything and anything. D.J., you take the west lookout; Joel, you take the Mayan Temple."

Hurray! Joel thought. I can watch for Vicky.

"Gary, Horace, and I will get things into shape around here," Marshall continued. "After we move the beds and gear, I want to board up these windows."

"You mean we'll have to sit in the dark?" D.J. exclaimed.

"Would you rather the windows blew in?" Horace teased.

"I don't want things blowing *through* the windows, either," Joel's father said. "Flying debris is one of the dangers."

"Do I have to *stay* out in the blind?" Joel cried, suddenly frightened.

His father gave him a scornful look, but D.J. said quickly, "Of course not! We stay out there till the men get the work done."

In the barracks Joel stuffed his clothes into suitcase and knapsack and rolled up his hammock. He picked up the clipboard and pencil he was taking to the blind. They'd kept his transistor in the kitchen.

At the door he hesitated. "What if the hurricane comes while I'm there?" he asked D.J.

She smiled. "You'll get plenty of warning," she promised. "The wind begins to blow harder and harder, that's all. I'll come get you before that happens. If this island is in the center of the eye, as it's called, the wind will stop after several hours and everything will get calm. Then the wind will come back from the opposite direction. Like an enormous spin cycle of a washing machine," she added. "If you can imagine a washing machine moving across the kitchen, and wind instead of water."

Not entirely comforted Joel set off for the Mayan Temple. He was really worried about Vicky. As he made his way through the dark warehouse, he tried to convince himself that as soon as he climbed the stairs and looked out he would see Vicky's boat.

Unfortunately the sea was empty. Joel trained his binoculars on the island. Nothing moved there. What if the light Gary saw meant someone had come for her? Maybe she wasn't even there.

The terns were stretching and preening, smoothing the damage to their feathers from last night's downpour. They didn't seem to expect a storm.

Low clouds were crossing the sky. The gray water was smooth, as smooth as he'd ever seen it, as if the pelting rain had beaten down the waves. A good time for Vicky to come. She shouldn't be on Little Rat, not in a bad storm. Water might rush right over it. The highest part wasn't very high. What should he do?

11

Rescue Mission

Joel looked at his watch. Eight thirty now. Two terns rose into the air, followed by a third. Another came in with a silversides in its beak. A fledgling ran from the grass and seized the fish. Joel made notes. If the chicks stayed in the thick grass, would the hurricane blow over them?

He kept wishing he could send Vicky a message. People fired shots, waved flags, flashed lights. Mirrors! People sometimes used mirrors. That might attract her attention.

Yesterday he could have gotten a mirror from the barracks. Gary had one; so did D.J. Now both were packed. A small green-framed one hung in the kitchen. If he could get that . . . He slid off the stool, grabbed the clipboard, and plunged down the dark stairs.

On the path the air seemed hot and muggy, the clouds lower than ever. He approached the kitchen with caution. If he ran into his father, what was his excuse? Ah . . . the ballpoint was out of ink! Considering everything, Vicky was causing him to do an awful lot of lying.

In the empty kitchen the transistor was yapping that the storm would hit New York about three o'clock. Offices should close early and people should go home. In the lab Gary and Horace were having trouble unfolding one of the cots.

Joel was slipping the mirror from its nail when he heard Gary say, "Let me get the hammer." When he came into the kitchen, Joel was taking bread from the breadbox, and the mirror lay hidden under the clipboard on the table.

"Aha!" Gary said. "You'll get fat again, if you keep that up."

"What do you mean 'again'?" Joel muttered.

"Well, nobody could call you fat now! You must've taken in your belt since you came, right?"

It was a strange moment for such a discovery. Joel was worried about the hurricane, worried about Vicky, worried his father would catch him away from his post, worried someone would notice the mirror. Yet the idea that he had lost weight—quite a lot—drove the rest from his mind.

He grinned unbelievingly, looking down at his stomach. "Have I?"

"Can't you tell?" Gary pulled out the end of Joel's belt. "Look, that's where you *were* wearing it."

"I thought it stretched," Joel stammered. "I don't feel any different."

"Well, you sure look different. Go on. A slice of bread won't hurt." He patted Joel on the head, a rare gesture for Gary.

The radio blared suddenly. *"If the hurricane continues in its present course, it will pass over eastern Long Island some time this afternoon—"*

"Cripes, that's us!" Gary cried. "Horace, you hear?" He hurried into the lab.

"—but," the announcer finished, *"the weather bureau this morning still hopes the storm will veer, swinging back out to sea and treating the coast to nothing more than drenching rains."*

Joel left the kitchen to the sound of hammering. He trotted back to the Mayan Temple, glancing down at himself on the way. His none-too-clean shirt hung straight. He wondered if his father had noticed. His face in the mirror looked thinner. Brown, too. Well, *something* should have happened. He hadn't had soda or potato chips since he left home.

Again he hoped to see Vicky's boat, but the sea was still empty. If she was leaving, she might have come by and told him.

The problem now was whether to tell his father. What if she was still on the island? What if the storm didn't come? Vicky would be mad if he gave her secret away for no reason. But if he waited and something bad happened, his father would be mad. Joel sighed. It was hard to know what to do. He stared at the terns. There were fewer; two swooped away while he watched.

Suddenly a solution occurred to him. He could run over to Little Rat while everybody was busy. No one would miss him. If Vicky was still there, he could bring her back and hide her in the Mayan Temple, if she didn't want to be seen. It would be safer than Little Rat. It was silly to sit here worrying when he could zip over there. Gary had been leaving the outboard on the boat lately. If it was still on the boat, he'd go. Vicky ran her boat alone. So could he.

A lot of terns had gone now. The ones hatching eggs or covering chicks were still on the job, though. He was making a note when he heard a faraway bark.

Sirius? He snatched up the binoculars. Sure enough— the cocker spaniel was bounding from rock to rock, barking toward Great Rat.

Joel climbed out of the lookout. Could the dog see him? He tried to flash the mirror, but it didn't work well. The sky was too dark. Poor dog! How could Vicky go off and leave him? Maybe she hadn't been able to hold him in the boat.

Joel traversed the storehouse again, climbed over the hill, and took the path along the rocks. Thus he avoided the kitchen. Over on Little Rat, Sirius was still barking.

The motor was attached to the boat. Now he really had to decide. But he *had* decided, back in the lookout; he was going to Little Rat. If Vicky was gone, he'd rescue Sirius.

Puffing, he shoved the boat into the water. What if he got caught now? He'd tell, that's all. But nobody came down the path. Surely Gary hadn't forgotten the boat.

The motor started. Joel steered into deep water before turning parallel to the shore. Even way out on the water he heard the echo of hammering. The men were boarding up the windows. He'd be back before they finished.

When he drew close to Little Rat, Sirius heard the motor and came flying over the boulders. Barking, he followed the boat's progress along the shoreline. Remembering their first meeting, Joel wondered if Sirius would actually get into the boat with him.

The water was becoming a little rough. Joel rounded the point on which the big building stood and turned the prow toward the strip of beach. Vicky's boat was there, under the low cliff on which the building stood.

Then he saw Vicky, waving frantically. She was sitting on the rocks at the far end of the beach. A wave hit the rocks, drenching her with spray. Why didn't she move? She must be caught!

Joel cut the motor, tilted it, and let momentum carry him in. A second glance at Vicky showed another wave breaking over her. Sirius was running back and forth on the sand, whining.

Joel rolled up his pant legs, jumped in, and beached the boat beside Vicky's. Then he sped toward her, Sirius ahead of him. She was blue-lipped and shivering, her blond hair drenched and dark.

"What's wrong?" he cried.

"My foot's caught," she said steadily, and then burst into tears. "Oh, why didn't you bring someone? You can't get me out. You're too little. I've been here hours!" she sobbed. "Since daylight."

"How'd you do it?"

"My foot slipped . . . I fell . . . All my weight came down on that leg and it slid down between the rocks, and my shoe's caught. I can't pull my leg out. I'm down here so far, there's nothing I can put my weight against." She wriggled to show him. "We need someone big, grown-up. You can't lift me."

"I can try." Joel locked his arms around her from behind and tugged, but she was right. He wasn't strong enough to pull her out. He let go and stepped back.

"I'd better go get someone."

She let out a wail. "No! Don't leave!"

"The tide's coming in," he shouted, stepping back as a wave splashed them both.

"It's in," she cried, wiping spray from her face. "It won't come any higher. Build a bonfire, so some boat will see us."

"There aren't any boats," Joel argued. He was about to add, "on account of the hurricane," but he didn't want to scare her. "It looks too much like rain," he said instead.

"Well, build a bonfire so they'll come over from Great Rat!"

"They can't," he said slowly. "I've got the boat." He realized with an awful sinking in his stomach that he'd done wrong not to tell his father. It wasn't safe for a person to camp alone on an island. "Vicky, I have to get them."

"No! *Please* don't leave. There must be some other way! If you could just move that rock—even an inch."

The granite boulder was the size of a big TV and much heavier. Joel studied it.

"I might be able to pry it loose." Before school ended, he had studied levers and fulcrums. Somebody a long time ago had bragged he could move the world if he could get a long enough lever. Joel only hoped it would work fast. The wind was coming up, and the waves were getting choppy. "I'll find something," he told Vicky. She nodded, shivering and hugging Sirius, who licked her face. Joel ran up the slope.

The huge windowless storehouse had double doors in the side facing the ocean. A cement runway had extended from the doors to a pier, but storm tides had destroyed the pier and most of the runway. Waves had cut away the rock-buttressed shore, leaving the cliff and the beach.

One half of the double door was rusted shut, but the other opened easily. Inside Joel could discern nothing—it was too dark. He closed the door and ran on, circling behind the building. In back he found a dead pine, its trunk no bigger than a fencepost. It stood upright, clinging to the rocky outcrop, but when he shoved, it fell, dirt clinging to its gnarled root. Stubs of branches remained at its other end, but maybe he could shove it down between the rocks.

He dragged it to the beach. Miraculously, the end fit the hole. The root end slanted high in the air. Joel leaped and clung to it with both hands. Dirt showered his hair.

"Ready!" he panted, and tugged with his whole body. He heard a crack. The trunk sagged, and he barely got out from under before it thumped to the ground.

"The rock was going to move," Vicky cried. "I felt it. Try again!"

Joel wedged the shortened pine trunk into the crack and tried. Nothing happened. It was too short now for leverage.

"It's no use," he puffed. "I'll have to find something else."

Vicky held her brow. "There're some pipes inside," she said wearily. "Joel. Maybe you *should* go for help."

Joel felt a great relief. "Let me try those pipes, and then I will." He ran to the building. It was still just as dark inside. He should have asked her which corner to look in. He found the pipes only because he stumbled over them. They were like the gas pipes in his mother's studio, and rusty. He picked up two and hauled them through the door. They were long, and side by side two might be stronger than one. If they didn't bend.

The pipes slid into the crack, standing straight, like rusty flagpoles, so he pulled them out until they sagged against the rock on which Vicky rested. Rust flakes cut into his hands.

"Okay, Vicky," he said when he had them where he thought they'd do the most good. "Be ready to move."

She braced her hands against the rock she sat on and placed her free foot against the rock.

"Okay, now!" He bent over the ends of the pipes, hauling down as hard as he could. The rock moved ever so slightly.

"It's coming," Vicky gasped, wriggling like a goldfish. "I'm out!" she cried. He saw a bare foot wave in the air. Vicky flopped on her back exhausted.

Joel eased up on the pipes and went to stand beside her.

"Oh," she shrieked, "my leg's full of pins and needles. Oh, Joel! You're a good friend. I never had such a good friend."

It was true, Joel thought, pleased with himself. He *was* a good friend. "What happened to your sneaker?" he asked. The rescue work wasn't over yet.

"It's down there. I worked my foot out of it."

"Can you stand up?" He held out his hand.

"I'll try." She clung to his outstretched hand and got to her feet. When she put her weight on her bare foot, she winced with pain. The wind blew through her wet clothing, and she wrapped her arms about her body. "I have to get dry clothes," she said through chattering teeth and limped toward the building.

Joel cast a glance at the sea, now frothing all along the rocks. He ran to catch up with her.

"Hurry," he urged. "We have to go."

"I just want to get warm. Would you make me some tea, or something?"

"There isn't time!" Joel cried. "There's a hurricane coming."

"Yeah," Vicky said. "I listened last night."

"Well, it's worse now," Joel insisted. "That's why I came. The water's going to blow right over this island."

"*This* island?"

"All water-level places. They're boarding up the windows at Great Rat."

"All right," she said.

She made him wait outside while she changed. It seemed to take ages. Probably because it was so dark inside. Joel jumped up and down on one foot. "Hurry," he shouted.

Finally she came out wearing dry blue jeans, two

sweaters, and a blue zippered sweatshirt with a hood. She was barefooted and her pant legs were rolled above the knees. Her teeth chattered again as the wind hit her. Joel was looking forward to getting in the boat and rolling down his own pant legs. He wished he'd worn a jacket, but it had been so hot before.

"Don't you want to take your stuff?" he asked Vicky.

She shook her head and limped off toward the boat. Sirius was waiting. Joel thought it wouldn't hurt to shut the open half of the big iron door. He clanged it closed and ran after her.

"What about your boat?" he asked when he came up. He wished she'd talk, be as cocky and bossy as she usually was.

Vicky shrugged. "It's too heavy to drag up that hill, and there's nothing to tie it to." She shrugged again.

Together they launched the aluminum boat, and the three of them splashed into it. The motor started right away. As Vicky began rolling down her pant legs, Joel looked at her with a grin, happy to be escaping. To his surprise tears were rolling down her face.

"What's the matter?" he shouted into the wind.

She wiped the tears away. "I'm so hungry! And cold!"

The waves had become awful. Joel realized how high they had risen when the boat began chugging through them. He'd never been on such rough water. The wind was coming straight at them, and the waves came in long, menacing hills. He wondered if it was safe. He wished Vicky would talk to him, but she was straddling the thwart, staring at the island. Was she sorry to be leaving?

Joel scarcely dared take his eyes off the oncoming waves. One crested beneath them and slapped them with spray. Vicky wiped her face dry. In one smooth movement she was beside him on the stern seat. To escape the spray, he thought.

Using her hand as a megaphone, she shouted at him: "We're not getting anywhere!"

At first Joel didn't understand what she meant. She saw the puzzlement in his face and pointed to the island. "It's the wind," she shouted in his ear. "The motor's not strong enough."

He tore his attention from the masses of gray water tumbling ahead of them and looked over his right shoulder. He could hardly believe it! Despite the horrific waves they had passed through, they were almost at the place where they'd entered the surf. The boat and Little Rat appeared to be drifting together through a sea violently racing the other way.

"We have to go back!" Vicky screeched in his ear.

How did one do that? Joel made a gesture of helplessness.

"Let me take it!" she shouted.

Willingly he relinquished the tiller. She knew about boats and didn't seem to be afraid even now (as he was). Looking at those tumbling dark waves, it seemed more sensible to him to take his chances on land. But it wouldn't be easy turning the boat around. He could imagine what would happen if one of those sliding gray hills caught them sideways.

Vicky was too wise to let them get caught. She ran

the motor just enough to keep their prow pointed into the waves. Then she let wind and waves carry them backwards, shorewards. At the perfect, smooth moment, she turned the boat's nose forty-five degrees. Choosing the right instant, she called upon the motor for all its power and brought them zooming in. They came to rest high on the little beach.

"Whew!" Joel said. "I'm glad we came back."

12

Isolated

Vicky stumbled out of the boat. "We'd better drag it inside, if we can!" she shouted. Joel noticed she was still shivering.

He unscrewed the clamps that held the outboard motor, but when he tried to lift it, he discovered how heavy it was. Vicky came to help. Together they carried it up the slope by the cliff and into the building.

"Put it here beside mine," she said in the comparative quiet. Joel perceived the shape of Vicky's outboard on the floor.

Then they went back for the boat.

Good thing it's no bigger, Joel thought, as they huffed and puffed to push it up the slope. Aluminum was amazingly heavy. It sounded dreadful, too, scraping across the stony ground. Halfway up they had to stop and rest.

Joel said, "I bet you're not cold now!" He himself was welcoming the cooling wind.

"No," Vicky said, but neither did she remove her jacket. They had to rest twice more before they finally got the boat to the door, tipped it sideways, and slid it in.

Just in time, too. A spatter of rain sang against the metal. Mist blew in Joel's face. Sirius rushed in, and Vicky shut the door. She dropped the iron bar in place.

"Now," she said with a sigh. "We can relax. My stuff's down here."

At one end of the building light came through slitted ventilators near the roof. Joel's nose wrinkled. The place smelled of old fires. His eyes accustomed themselves to the dimness, and he saw, under the ventilator, Vicky's things—sleeping bag, kerosene camp stove "borrowed" from her grandfather's boathouse, a row of canned food, water jug, gasoline for the outboard.

She lit the camp stove, poured water into a pan, and set it to heat.

"You want hot chocolate?" she asked Joel.

"You have milk?" he exclaimed.

"I make it with water. It's okay."

"Sure," Joel said. He was hungry, ready for more than hot chocolate.

As though reading his mind, Vicky offered him bread and peanut butter and a knife.

The sandwich he made tasted delicious. He looked around the place while he ate. "It's dark in here," he said finally. "Gloomy."

"I just sleep here," she explained.

"How come you didn't come to Great Rat before this?" Joel asked her.

"I meant to," she said, "but before I knew it, it was past eight o'clock, both mornings. The time just slipped by."

"Gary saw a light here last night," Joel said. "Was it you?"

"No, a boat tied up on the other side."

"I thought they'd come to get you and Sirius got left behind."

"No chance!" Vicky hugged the dog, who was lolling beside her.

"He was out on the rocks this morning, barking at Great Rat," Joel explained. "That's why I came over."

"Thank you, Sirius," Vicky said, kissing the top of his head.

Something whooshed and rattled on the roof. Joel gave a startled glance upwards.

"Rain," Vicky said with a shiver. "I'm glad we're at this end. The storm's coming from that way." She pointed to the other end.

The water in the pan was bubbling. Vicky poured it into a cup and a bowl, spooned in powder, and set the cup before Joel.

"Let's listen to the radio," Joel said.

Vicky turned it on. The announcer was still talking about the hurricane. He told what the high water was doing in Atlantic City, what was happening in New York, what was likely to happen on Long Island, Connecticut, even Boston.

"It's too much," Vicky said. She turned the dial, but all the other stations were saying the same thing. "Do you want to hear any more?" she asked. "I'm not sure how much battery's left."

"No," Joel said. The things the announcer said had frightened him, too. He wished his father knew where he was. He should have left a note. But he hadn't thought he'd be gone long! By now they must have discovered that the boat was missing. They might have discovered he was missing, too.

"Do you mind if I get into my sleeping bag?" Vicky's question broke into his thoughts. "It's so cold." She slid into the bag. "Aren't you cold?"

"No." The rain on the roof sounded cold, but the air still felt warm.

"You can wear my wool poncho, if you want to," Vicky told him. "It's over there with my clothes. You know what else you could do—if you don't like the dark?" She lay with her head propped on one elbow. "You could build a fire. Where those rocks are—see? I built a hearth."

Joel peered through the gloom at a circle of blackened rocks near the foot of Vicky's sleeping bag.

"There's no chimney," he protested. "You can't build a fire in the house."

"Yes, you can! The smoke all goes up to the ceiling and out through those slits. Like an Iroquois longhouse."

"Do you have wood?"

"Over by the wall. Would you want to go out and get more? Before it gets wet?"

"Sure," Joel said with alacrity. He didn't like the dimness.

"You can wear my rain poncho," Vicky offered. "It's all folded up someplace."

First, Joel thought, he'd cross the island to where he could see Great Rat. Maybe they'd be looking for him.

He sighed. His father would have all the time the hurricane lasted to get madder and madder. He would certainly punish him. Maybe send him to his grandmother's or some camp! Just when he was getting used to everything on Great Rat, too. He put on the rain poncho and started for the door. Sirius rose from Vicky's sleeping bag and followed.

"Come on, boy," Joel said, low-voiced. Vicky looked as though she might be asleep.

Joel welcomed the gray light. Wind tore at the poncho, but the rain had stopped. Masses of dirty clouds filled the sky. The air felt charged with electricity. As they reached the corner of the building, another shower came driving in from the sea, splattering them with cold drops.

The island was one big rock. Over the centuries the cracks had collected enough soil to nurture scrubby pine trees. The trees thrust their roots into the cracks and dropped their needles to form a thick mat. Among the pines the wind wasn't so strong, though Joel could hear it whistling overhead. The shower blew over.

The pines didn't seem to shed their dead limbs. He saw some he could have pulled down, but he didn't want to take the time. He planned to look among the rocks for driftwood, pieces of board that would burn neatly.

When he came to the edge of the trees and looked across the stretch of rioting water, Great Rat looked as barren as when he'd first seen it. He waded through the low bushes at the edge of the trees and waved his arms. Nothing happened. He could see no sign of life over there. Not even terns. Hadn't they missed him?

The waves were splashing high on the rocks. In the open the wind was fierce. Sirius was capering about and sniffing. Stupid dog! Why couldn't he bark now?

Joel saw a piece of driftwood at the edge of the bushes, and another, and another. They all seemed quite dry. As he bent to pick them up, the poncho blew over his head. He fought it down, but it blew up again. It happened three times before he managed to keep it where it belonged and pick up the wood, too. Then a savage gust threatened to blow him over the boulders. His hair whipped his face, and salt spray stung his eyes. He could hardly keep his balance long enough to look again at Great Rat.

Another squall hurtled across the open sea, obliterating Great Rat and the foam-lathered water. Joel was forced to retire to the shelter of the trees.

He and Sirius made their way through the woods to the side away from the wind. There he was finally able to gather a full armload of wood.

Entering the building was like entering a cave, so quickly did the walls muffle the wind. Joel welcomed the dimness as a relief from being buffeted. He piled the wood near the fireplace. Vicky didn't stir, and he tiptoed out to bring in a second load.

He collected a third load before driving rain sent him and Sirius scurrying inside for good. He glanced at Vicky then, wishing she'd wake up. Sirius made him self-conscious, always eyeing him. But Vicky didn't even stir.

For a while he watched the storm from the open door. Rain blew past in sheets, which wasn't too awful. He'd seen it rain like that in New York. But when the rain ceased for an instant, he caught a glimpse of rolling gray water surging almost to the top of the cliff! Several feet of water must be washing over the beach; Vicky's boat would be gone.

Joel imagined himself at the edge of the cliff, looking down. What if the wind hurled him into that turbulent gray-and-white mass? A person couldn't swim in water like that. He saw himself flung this way and that before sinking once and for all.

He slammed the door shut with a clang, forgetting Vicky, and dropped the bar. No sense in keeping the poncho on. He stripped it off and laid it across Gary's boat. Good thing he and Vicky had brought that boat in! At least Gary wouldn't be mad at him.

He tiptoed across the floor. Vicky moaned, but she didn't wake up, even when he whispered her name.

Sighing at bearing all the worry alone—the storm, his father—he set about building a fire. Sirius watched. Joel collected matches, paper, and twigs. *Indian build small fire and stand close,* he remembered. *White man build big fire and stand far away.* Well, he, Joel, wasn't going to build a big fire in here!

The fire he built was so little it burned up the three twigs and went out. He had to make another start, being bolder about adding wood, and soon had a blaze crackling cheerily. It threw a heartwarming light over everything.

Wind-driven rain pelted the roof, and gusts of wind seemed to shake the building, but the fire held the forces of Nature at bay. Joel was kept busy tending it, almost too busy to think about how his father must feel. They must all be wondering what had become of him.

He made more hot chocolate and sat cross-legged, pretending to be an Iroquois.

The noise outside became one deep-throated roar, like city traffic only a hundred times louder. He turned on the radio. That was better, until a bulletin said the full fury of the hurricane would soon strike Long Island and tides would be eleven feet above normal.

Something heavy thudded on the roof. Sirius laid back his ears and gave a sharp bark. What was his problem? With a *woof!* he came and collapsed beside Joel. The noise on the roof had scared him, too.

The radio sounded tiny and lost. Joel turned it off. The wind, the thunder of the surf grew louder.

He was about to fix himself another peanut butter sandwich when a movement from Vicky caught his eye. She was sitting up, staring at the fire.

"It's hot in here!" she exclaimed. "Why don't you open a window?"

"A window!" Joel cried. "What are you talking about?"

"Oh!" She seemed to realize where she was. "I don't know. It's so hot!" She crawled out of the sleeping bag and lay atop it.

"Are you hungry?" Joel asked. "Do you want a sandwich?"

"No. But I'd love a drink of water."

Joel poured water into the plastic tumbler he found beside the water jug. She drank it and asked for more.

"My head aches," she fretted. Tears filled her eyes

and spilled over. She lay down with her head on her arm. "I wish this was over. I want to go home." Her eyes closed, and she seemed to fall asleep.

Joel went back to tending the fire. Vicky ought to stay awake and talk. It was her fault he was here. If he hadn't come, she might still be caught in those rocks.

His stomach tightened as he realized those rocks were covered with water. She'd have drowned! Her fine blonde hair, fanned now on the sleeping bag, would be washing back and forth in the waves. He shuddered. What made him keep thinking of horrible things? He jumped to his feet and walked around.

He went to the door, intending to look out, but the wind in its fury was rattling the heavy iron frame as though it were a garbage can lid. If he opened the door, he might not be able to close it again. So he peered through the crack instead. He could see very little. The blowing rain was thick as fog. The ground beside the cement slab was swept clean. Not a pebble remained. Even the rain seemed to blow away as fast as it fell. Then, while he watched, a flood of white surf rolled across it. The tide! It had come this high!

This was what the radio had been predicting. He pressed his face to the crack. Another wave rolled over the receding one, splashing the doorstep.

How high was eleven feet? The question was urgent. When he'd stood on the beach, the top of the cliff had been only a foot or two above his head. So the cliff was how high? Maybe six feet. That meant the tide might rise five feet higher. Would it come into the building?

The rusty doors weren't watertight. He could see daylight all around them.

He glanced toward their camp, everything spread on the floor. The fire flickered and Joel ran to replenish it. No sense in letting it go out.

He was returning to the door when a new sound attracted his attention—a kind of gurgle underfoot. Looking down, he saw a square iron grating in the cement. A drain. The gurgle came from it, and that gurgle was seawater. If the tide kept rising, the drains would let water in instead of out. The whole floor would be flooded —Vicky's sleeping bag, the fire, everything. There'd be no place to get away from it.

13

Flood Tide

Joel tried to look out again, but he could see no further than the foam-laced water splashing the doorstep. Rain and blowing spray obscured everything else.

He ran back to turn on the radio. Only then did he realize the screaming intensity of the gale. Unless he held the radio to his ear, he could hear nothing. It wasn't the battery, either, because when he shouted to Sirius, he could hardly hear his own voice.

He shut the radio off and turned to the drains. He could see water below the gratings, and there was nothing around to plug them up with. The only thing to do was move, but where? The hill outside—with the wind blowing eighty miles an hour—was out of the question.

He looked ceilingward, wishing for a second story or some kind of perch. He knew a painter who'd built a high platform in his loft, with a ladder leading to it. Lowering his gaze, he caught sight of Gary's boat, upside down near the door. They could move into the boat! Boats floated, on ocean or bathtub. The idea of sitting in a boat, inside a building, was so crazy he had to laugh. Nevertheless, they could make themselves comfortable in it, even sleep in the bottom, all tight and dry. A good thing they'd brought it in!

He went to inspect it and struggled to turn it right side up. The noise he made was hardly noticeable above the scream of the wind. Rain or spray was blowing through the ventilator. He managed to drag the boat toward the fire, but it was hard to handle alone. He wished Vicky wouldn't be so lazy.

He went to where she lay. "Vicky!" He knelt to shake her arm and drew his hand back in surprise. She was hot!

"Vicky!"

She rolled her head and moaned. Sirius looked to Joel for explanation.

"Vicky. Are you sick?" He put his hand on her forehead the way his mother felt his forehead before saying he had a fever. He guessed Vicky had a fever, all right. She felt awfully hot. She tossed her head and cried that he was hurting her.

It was up to him. He had to get everything into the boat as soon as possible. The water might come in fast. When it did, it would put out the fire and they'd be in the dark. It was best to do things while there was still some light.

The first consideration was food and water. What about Sirius? He was probably hungry now. Joel found the box of dog kibble and poured some on the floor. Sirius didn't seem to mind the informality. He might be thirsty, too. The gallon jug was over half full of water and there was

another full one, as well. Joel found the cut bottom half
of still another jug. Was that Sirius's dish? Joel splashed
water into it and turned to the task of moving camp.

He took Vicky's clothes and her knapsack to the boat.
She could stretch out in the front two-thirds if she was
still sick. She'd have the sleeping bag to lie on. He'd
take the stern. He set about making himself a nest.

The boat had drained while it lay upside down. Now
he used Vicky's bathtowel to finish drying it. It tilted to
one side because of the keel, the long central rib under-
neath, but he guessed they could manage. If water did
come in to float it, it would be level. He spread news-
papers first, then Vicky's clothing, then her poncho
on top. It was a pretty thin nest; he could feel the ribs of
the boat through it, but it was better than cold metal.

Next he carried the camp stove to the boat and set it
on the stern seat. Would it be risky to use it? The boat
wouldn't be tossing about; it would be like floating in a
swimming pool.

He turned his attention to food. The bread he'd take,
and the peanut butter, of course, and the box of powdered
milk. But what about the cans of stuff? He decided it
wouldn't hurt them to get wet, and they'd take up space
in the boat. He put in a can of stew and a can of peaches,
in case. Among the food he found four white candles.
"Hurray," he said to himself. "The very thing!" He put
them and the tin of matches in his jacket pocket.

All the food that the water might hurt could be stowed
neatly under the stern seat, he found. It was kind of fun
putting things together like that, if it weren't so scarey,

too. They could be setting out for a real voyage. *The owl and the pussycat put to sea, in a beautiful pea-green boat.*

He looked around the floor. What else did he have to do? He piled more wood on the fire so he could see. The water in the drains didn't seem to be rising. He went to take another look outside. Gray water, full of sand and seaweed, was splashing the steps, but not much worse than before.

Gary's motor! He managed to lug it to the boat and attach it, tilted, so the blades wouldn't scrape the floor. Too bad about the other outboard. Getting soaked probably wouldn't be good for it, but there was no room for it in the boat.

Everything was set. All he had to do now was move Vicky. He'd even cut off a piece of the painter so they could tie Sirius in the boat. It wouldn't do for the dog to be jumping in and out.

There was one more thing—Joel was hungry. He opened a can of beans and set it in the fire. There seemed to be time, since the water still hadn't risen any more. Maybe he'd moved things for nothing.

Next it sounded as though the wind had died. Joel listened. He couldn't hear a thing! His ears grew accustomed to the quiet, and he began to hear the surf. The high steady shriek had stopped. He no longer felt he was in the world's largest subway train rushing through the world's largest tunnel. He peered through the crack in the door.

Water slopped at the step. Cautiously he lifted the bar—a good bar, holding the door against anything the storm could do.

The scene outside was frightening. From horizon to horizon leaping gray water covered everything. The sky was still a mass of dirty clouds. The building seemed to float alone, like Noah's ark. But the wind had stopped.

He felt a need to wade around to the back of the building. The land had to be there; it was uphill. And now that the wind had died, he could build a fire they could see on Great Rat. As soon as the water settled down, he could return. He'd be so glad to get back, he wouldn't care how mad his father was.

He tied Sirius inside to stay dry. Rolling up his pant legs and putting on his wet sneakers, he set out. The tide was running strong, but it didn't come above his ankles. He followed the wall around to the back and clambered up the rocky hillside. The air felt sultry and oppressive, not crisp, the way it usually did after a storm.

Two fairly big trees had blown down. They lay wedged against the others. Great spaces of rock had been swept bare of needles, as though by a vacuum cleaner.

On the other side of the island, he found tossing waves where the bushes had been. The sky over Great Rat was almost clear.

In a nearby pine something moved. A black bird sat there, watching him. It had a thick bill, like a parrot's. It didn't look like any of the pictures of birds he had seen. He memorized it to describe to his father. It flitted to another tree, and Joel looked back at Great Rat. Still

no one outside, but maybe someone would be looking around soon. He started back to the building to get paper and matches.

A breeze from the opposite direction tossed his hair. It seemed to herald what looked like a low bank of fog rolling in. Then he remembered D.J. had talked about the middle of a hurricane—the eye. Was this the middle? The fogbank looked ominous. Something about it urged Joel to take to his heels. He sprang down the rock and splashed around the building. The wind came at him like a solid force. It seemed to suck the breath from his lungs. Without the wall to steady him, he'd have blown off his feet. As it was, he was hurled through the doorway. A last glimpse showed him that the oncoming wall wasn't fog at all. It was rolling, surging water! He needed all his strength to bar the door against the wind's renewed fury.

Recovering his breath, he ran to wake Vicky. He grabbed her hands and pulled her to a sitting position.

"Come on," he cried. "We have to get in the boat."

"The boat?" She looked around vaguely.

"Yes! Get up!"

She began to slide out of the sleeping bag.

"Come on," he urged. "We don't have much time."

"Where?"

"Over here." He bundled the sleeping bag under one arm and pushed her along with the other.

"I feel so sick," she grumbled. "Why are we here?"

"Just get in the boat," he coaxed, "then I'll explain."

She made fretful sounds while he spread the sleeping

bag, but she did as she was told.

"Do you want another drink?" he shouted. The rising noise muffled his voice. As he poured water for her, he remembered the beans. He handed her the tumbler quickly.

"I'll be back," he cried and sped to the fire. Rain was blowing through the ventilator at the opposite end now, making the fire hiss.

Joel splashed through the flood, careful not to spill hot bean juice. His sneakers were already wet, so getting them wet again didn't matter. He was very hungry. Where had he stowed the spoon?

He set the can of beans and his wet sneakers on the center thwart and climbed into the boat barefooted. Fumbling in his pockets, he pulled out a candle. He had trouble lighting it, because the building was full of drafts, but at last the wick caught. He stuck the candle to the boat's bottom, under the thwart. The flame blew about a lot, but it stayed lit. The thwart would be their little table, once he took his shoes off. He moved them to the foot of Vicky's sleeping bag.

She had crawled into it, and Sirius lay beside her. Joel could see their eyes shining in the candlelight.

"What's happening?" she asked fuzzily.

"The storm's coming back," Joel said. "Are you hungry?"

"No. Are we going home?"

Joel stared at her, a little frightened. She must be very sick! She didn't understand why they were in the boat.

140

"We're not going anywhere," he said at last.

He ate the beans and reached out to feel how high the water was. The boat shifted with a scraping sound. It must be nearly afloat.

"Vicky," he called. "Move over to the middle."

"Why?" she grumbled.

"To balance the boat."

"Why didn't you say so!" she demanded crossly.

He didn't bother to answer. She didn't seem to know what she was saying. But she shifted, and the boat was floating.

He found the radio, turned it on, and wished he hadn't. They were telling about people who'd drowned. The howling, screaming wind echoed inside the huge building.

Joel could tell from the way the boat rocked that Vicky was tossing about in her sleeping bag. But he was surprised when she sat up suddenly and faced him across the candlelight.

"Why are you doing this?" she demanded. "It's crazy!"

Joel was taken aback. "What should I have done?" he gasped.

"You should have stayed in camp!"

"In camp!" he echoed. What was the matter with her? He drew back from her and felt the stern thwart behind him. His face must have faded from the circle of candlelight.

"Where are you?" she wailed.

He didn't answer, and she lay down again.

He blew out the candle, so she couldn't see, and slowly his fear subsided. He began to hope she'd gone back to sleep. No, darn it, she was crying!

"Vicky?" he called. "Vicky, I'm here!"

After that she was quiet.

Joel sat wakeful and worried. He didn't know what made people go crazy, but it must have been dreadful for her being trapped in the rocks, watching the water rising. What if he and she were trapped here until they both went crazy? What if his father and Vicky's father came with a big boat and found their children had turned insane? *Then* they'd be sorry! Professor Marshall Curtis would be sorry he hadn't been nicer to his little boy, and Vicky's father would be sorry he hadn't let her go to Owens Island.

Then Joel had a worse thought: what if he had to be the one to explain to Vicky's father how she came to be here? He'd get blamed for not telling on her.

It was unfair! Tears sprang to his eyes and rolled down his cheeks unchecked. There was no one to see. Nobody appreciated him—not even Vicky.

Something cold and wet touched his bare foot. For an instant he was petrified. Then he felt a paw on his ankle. It was Sirius—trying to come to Joel's end of the boat.

Joel untied the rope from his collar. The dog wasn't going to jump out now. Instead, he curled against Joel, as if to give comfort. Joel wiped his face on his sleeve and gave Sirius a hug.

He spread Vicky's rain poncho over both of them and lay down, curled round the dog's warm, furry body. The hurricane had to end sometime. Maybe in the morning Vicky would be all right.

14

Rescue

Joel lay curled luxuriously in his hammock in the bar-racks—warm, safe, and dry. It must be nearly morning, but rain was blowing in. Something cold was sprinkling his face. He put a hand to his cheek and realized he wasn't in his hammock. And there was Sirius curled against him. He was still in Gary's boat! Disappointment surged over him. The spray on his cheek was blowing through the ventilator. But the wind wasn't so loud. He thought he could hear surf. Saddened by reality, he lost himself again in sleep.

When he woke next time, he could hear the surf, and he realized he was uncomfortable. His eyes flew open. He could see light through the ventilator. His discomfort was caused by the tilted boat resting on the floor. The water had gone down!

He rolled out of the boat, and Sirius jumped after him. The wind had stopped. The hurricane was surely over!

Vicky still slept, and Joel just left her. He felt he couldn't get outside fast enough.

When he opened the door, he saw that the flood tide had dropped, leaving the rocky ground looking scoured. Waves still splashed the clifftop, though, and the sea was still tempestuous.

Vicky was awake when he went back in.

"Feel any better?" he asked.

She shook her head. "It hurts to breathe," she croaked.

"Do you want to get up?"

"No." She began to cough.

Joel decided she had the flu.

He fixed hot chocolate, and when they were sipping it, he said, "I'm going to build a bonfire, so my father'll know I'm here. We might not be able to get there this morning—"

Vicky shook her head. A bout of coughing overcame her. "Oh, Joel," she managed to say, "I think I'm awful sick."

"All the more reason to go," Joel said.

"We . . . *can't* go," she gasped between coughs. "The water stays . . . rough . . . for days."

Joel felt a coldness that had nothing to do with the morning's chill.

"You mean we have to stay here!" he exclaimed. "But you need a doctor!"

Vicky nodded miserably.

"I'll build a fire," he reasoned. "When they see the smoke, they'll do something."

"What?"

What could they do? They didn't have a boat or a telephone or anything on Great Rat. "They'll think of something," he said.

Vicky shook her head. "Build a fire out there." She pointed toward the door.

"In front? No one will see it," Joel objected.

Vicky lay back, breathing in shallow gasps. "A boat . . . might. Watch! If one comes, flap your arms. That's . . . signal," she said weakly. "Please. I *know!*" She closed her eyes, and tears ran from under her lids.

Joel thought over her words. In one way he was glad she was bossy again. She seemed more like herself. But he wanted to build a fire on the other side, so his father would see it and he, Joel, could stop feeling guilty. But it was true, no one over there could help them. And the boats did pass on this side. He had to admit Vicky knew about boats and the sea. She should. She spent all her summers on an island.

"Okay," he said finally, "if you think it'll work."

"Flap your arms," she repeated, "if you see a boat."

Making a fire was harder than Joel had expected. He got paper from the bottom of the boat, but all the wood in the building was watersoaked. All the driftwood outside was afloat in the high tide. The dead branches had been snapped off the trees and blown probably to Connecticut. However, the two trees that had blown down were not too big to move. With perseverance he was able to drag one of them down to the front of the building and break the remaining limbs by jumping on them. If he could get a fire going, the damp wood would smoke a lot, which was what he wanted.

With Vicky's knife he whittled a pile of slivers for kindling and built the fire against the pine trunk. White smoke billowed up. His eyes searched the empty ocean. Now all he had to do was wait.

He kept the fire small. It wouldn't do to burn all the wood, but that meant tending it constantly so it wouldn't go out. When he had a moment, though, he did take time to fetch a can of stew to heat in the coals.

And all the time he was watching.

He ate the stew, and by then he saw he would need the other tree. Not because the first one had burned up, but in order to get it to burn well at all. His grandfather had taught him that logs burned better laid side by side. So he brought the second and laid the tree trunks that way, and it worked.

Once he thought he saw a boat far out in the waves. But it didn't reappear. It might just have been another whitecap. He reported to Vicky when he had a chance, but she didn't respond much. It would have been good to have someone to talk to, even though the need to be constantly stoking the fire made the morning pass quickly. He could only add wet wood a piece at a time.

By afternoon he was tired of the whole business. The waves were flinging themselves as high as ever. He'd have let the fire burn out, except it was a way of passing time. Moreover, he didn't want to report to Vicky that her idea had failed.

He was just staring wistfully at the leaping horizon when suddenly a new movement caught the corner of his eye. He whirled. It was a big boat—more like a ship —and it was coming around the island, so close in he could see the people in the wheelhouse.

He leaped to his feet and began flapping his arms— up and down, up and down—as Vicky had urged him, although he felt pretty silly.

Once again Vicky was right. The signal worked. A bell rang, and the boat reversed engines, or something. He could see a man in an officer's cap looking at him through binoculars.

Joel ran to the door. "Here's a boat!" he called triumphantly. "Come out!"

Vicky appeared in the doorway, coughing. "Coast Guard cutter," she croaked. "Oh, Joel! We'll be all right now."

Indeed, from that moment their worries were over, although their rescue seemed to take place in slow motion. The boat crossed in front of them, turned, came back. Vicky interpreted its movements. "The captain's looking for a landing place."

Something dark gray was dropped into the sea.

"Rubber dinghy," Vicky said.

Two men wearing orange life preservers climbed into the dinghy and started its outboard motor. They made for the rocky ledge in front of the children.

Sirius stood back from the waves and barked until Joel caught him and gave him to Vicky to hold. Then Joel went to the edge of the cliff, to wait. If they threw him a line, he would haul the dinghy in.

147

They did. Joel caught it, feeling sailorly, and held it taut, as the men waited their chance. When a wave tossed the boat level with the shelf of rock, one man leaped. He sprawled near Joel and picked himself up. He was wearing a rubber suit like a diver.

"Hello, son. Don't you like being Robinson Crusoe?" With a friendly grin, he took the line from Joel. The other man jumped, missed his footing and fell into the waves. The first coastguardsman hauled him dripping onto the rock. Thanks to his rubber suit, he didn't seem to mind the dunking.

"Now, what's your problem?" the first man asked.

"She's sick," Joel pointed to Vicky.

"You kids here alone?"

"Yes." Joel started to explain, but the first coastguardsman, who introduced himself as Simpson, said, "Take a look at her, Red, while I look for a place to rig onto." He ran off uphill behind the building.

"Where's he going?" Joel asked, following Red to where Vicky huddled on the doorstep.

"We're going to rig what's called a breeches buoy to get you off," Red explained. He felt Vicky's forehead and counted her pulse. "This girl's under the weather, all right. Nothing to worry about, though," he told Vicky. "We'll get you on board and give you penicillin. You'll be on the mend before you reach the hospital."

Vicky tried to speak, but Red shushed her. He scooped her up, carried her inside and tucked her into the sleeping bag. "You stay quiet," he said with authority. "Your brother can do the talking."

"Come on," he said to Joel. "Outside."

"I'm not her brother," Joel told him. "We're friends. I came over to get her before the hurricane. It's a good thing I did! She was caught in those rocks out there, and I had to free her. Then it was so late we couldn't get back."

"So you spent the hurricane here? You look in pretty good shape!"

Joel nodded, pleased with himself. "My boat's inside. When the water came in the building, Vicky and I slept in it."

"Hasn't anyone missed you? The captain only came this way 'cause he saw smoke."

"They don't know where I am." Joel hung his head. "Vicky ran away from camp, and it was a secret."

"You mean that little girl was camping here alone?" Red shook his head in amazement.

"All I meant to do when I came was get the dog," Joel explained. "I thought she'd gone."

"Wait a minute. You're going too fast," Red said. "Where did you come from?"

"Great Rat. That's that island over there, where my father is. I took their boat, and they don't know where I am."

"Boy!" Red stared down at Joel. "I wouldn't like to be in your shoes!"

Joel bit his lip. But Red laughed as if it wasn't the end of the world.

Simpson came running around the corner. "Stand back in the doorway," he ordered Joel. "Out of the way."

A sound like a shot came from the boat, followed by a puff of smoke. A yellow rope came zinging in. It fell near the men. Simpson jumped on it and waved, then he and Red began to haul it in.

Joel couldn't figure out what good a little thin rope could do, but the men pulled and pulled, and presently Joel saw it was pulling two thicker ropes. Where they were tied to the yellow one, a sort of dufflebag was hanging. Simpson tied the thick ropes to the tree he'd chosen and unpacked the bag and fastened up a pulley.

"That's called a breeches buoy," Red explained, "because you sit in it like a pair of pants. We're going to put your little girlfriend in there and give her a nice ride—"

"She's not my girlfriend!" Joel protested.

"Sorry, your friend. Think you can take the dog?"

Joel eyed the dangling bag. "I guess so."

"Does he bite?"

Joel shrugged. "I don't know."

Red tenderly helped Vicky into her warmest clothes and carried her up the hill. She looked bright-eyed and pink-cheeked, but Red said that was the fever. "This is going to be the ride of your life," he told her.

The canvas bag came close to swallowing her. Her blue-jeaned legs and sneakers dangled from the two holes in the bottom. Her blue hooded jacket and the oval of her face appeared over the top. Simpson signaled the boat. Vicky waved. The next moment she sailed away like a shirt on a clothesline.

Joel and the coastguardsmen watched the people at

the other end remove her from the buoy.

"What will they do with her now?" Joel asked.

"Put her in sick bay," Red told him. "Couple of weeks from now she'll be camping again."

"She might be," Joel agreed. He wondered if they'd let her stay on Owens Island. If they didn't, he might never see her again!

"Okay, son, you're next," Simpson said. "I don't trust that dog, though, if he gets scared. Better put a muzzle on him, Red."

While Simpson pulled the line that brought the buoy back, Red tore a strip from Vicky's bathtowel and tied it like a bandage around Sirius's muzzle, knotting it behind his ears.

Sirius rolled his eyes. Joel, a little frightened himself at the idea of being suspended over that leaping water, was glad to busy himself comforting Sirius.

"Your turn, son." Before Joel could protest, Red popped him into the bag and put Sirius in his arms.

Joel's legs didn't fill up the holes, but the space left wasn't big enough for Sirius to fall through. The dog sat more or less on Joel's lap.

"How will you guys get back?" Joel questioned.

"When we get you over, we'll untie the rope and pull ourselves in, hand over hand." Red grinned at him.

Joel didn't believe it. They'd come back in the rubber boat.

Simpson signaled for the journey to begin. "See you on board!" he shouted.

With a jerk the buoy began to move. The seat swung

like one of the rides at Coney Island. As long as the rocks of the island were still beneath Joel's feet, the trip didn't seem so bad. But then he was traveling over the water. Foam-flecked gray waves splashed up, and his stomach leaped into his throat every time he looked down. Fortunately the ship, trim and white, was growing closer and closer. What would happen when he got on board? He forgot his fear of the water in wondering whether the captain would be very mad. Minutes later he was standing on deck, and Sirius, relieved of his muzzle, was frisking about.

"Welcome aboard," said a man with braid on his cap. "Your lady friend's going to the hospital. What are we going to do with you?"

While the ship waited for Simpson and Red to come aboard, Joel explained how he'd come over from Great Rat expecting to pick up the dog and go back.

"So you belong to that bunch of birdwatchers?" the captain said.

"They're scientists," Joel said. "My father's a professor."

"That explains it," one of the other men said with a laugh.

"I expect they'd like to have you back," the captain said. He turned to another officer. "Great Rat has a halfway decent beach. Are Red and Simpson fit for another trip? They can put this lad ashore in the raft."

Joel's heart swelled. Imagine being brought home by a Coast Guard cutter! And then in a rubber raft!

"Take him down to the galley," the captain ordered.

A red-cheeked man wearing a black cap led Joel away. The galley turned out to be a place to get soda. While Joel was there, Red and Simpson came in, still in their rubber suits.

"I hear we're taking you for another ride," Red said. Joel nodded.

"Did he tell you what a good job he did, sir, taking care of himself and that girl?" Red asked the black-capped man.

The man nodded. "His father ought to be proud of him. The girl's parents should be grateful, too."

Would his father be proud of him? Joel choked on the soda. The idea was too fantastic. But the captain thought his father would be glad to have him back. That could be true. A captain was supposed to know everything.

15

Safe Return

Joel supposed the Coast Guard would drop him off before Vicky, because Great Rat was closer. So he finished his soda as fast as he could and hurried on deck, only to see Great Rat and Little Rat disappearing astern. Red told him the ship was making for Long Island, to get Vicky to the hospital.

They entered the harbor and came alongside a pier where an ambulance was waiting. The ship had radioed ahead. Someone was going to telephone Owens Island, too, and a sailor promised to deliver Sirius to the Orient Yacht Club, to be picked up and taken home.

Vicky was carried down the gangplank on a stretcher, looking very small and limp. When Red came back aboard, he gave Joel a playful punch on the shoulder.

"Stop looking so glum, pal!" he said.

"Is she going to die?" Joel asked.

"Die! Of course not."

"How come she was on a stretcher, then? And the ambulance?"

"That's what stretchers are for, to carry sick people. And ambulances, too. Do you think we should have made her walk?"

"No." Joel had to smile.

The cutter backed away from the pier and headed for Great Rat. When they came near, Joel saw a bonfire burning there, too, though not such a good, smokey one as he himself had built.

By the time the cutter stood off from the rocky beach, four figures had gathered. Joel tried to pull himself above the railing so his father could see him. Red noticed and gave him a boost, holding him so Joel had a hand free to wave. Joel saw his father raise his binoculars.

The result was dramatic. The little party on shore had been standing dejectedly, simply watching the ship come to a stop. Then Marshall Curtis shouted to the others, pointed, and waved. Tearing off his binoculars, he handed them to Horace. Horace looked through them and waved, too. D.J. began jumping up and down. Gary took the glasses from Horace. Joel's father put a hand to his eyes and sat down on a rock, arms on knees. After a minute he took out his handkerchief. *Was he crying?* Joel began to feel very guilty.

Meanwhile, the rubber raft had gone over the side. Simpson, Red, and, last of all, Joel climbed down the ladder, Joel gripping the railings so hard his hands hurt. Red had found him a big, faded Coast Guard sweatshirt, and he'd been buckled into a life vest, but otherwise he had to wear his own clothes. From the way the sea was splashing about, he was going to get pretty wet. The ship was rising and falling at the same time the raft was falling and rising. Red plucked him from the end of the ladder, and together they toppled into the rubber bottom.

The motor was going, so Simpson just had to set the raft in motion and steer beachward. Joel waved a grateful farewell to the captain and the men leaning over the rail, then faced forward.

The trip in the inflated raft was wilder than a ride on a roller coaster. Every time a wave crested beneath them, they seemed to shoot out into midair. Then the raft almost fell out from under as they slid down into the trough. Joel was too busy hanging on and catching his breath to look where they were going. He wondered how Simpson could balance so calmly at the tiller. Once when there was a breathing space, Red rubbed Joel's head and grinned at him. Joel wiped salt water from his face and returned a sickly smile.

Moments later the bottom of the raft scraped rock. Simpson cut the engine. Red leaped out to pull them in. And there stood his father, with D.J., Gary, and Horace behind him.

Then his father was hugging him with both arms. For once, he'd laid his binoculars aside. The others were shaking hands with Red and Simpson, and everyone was talking at once. Red told how the Coast Guard had seen Joel's bonfire and removed the children from the island.

"But who's Vicky?" Joel's father asked, bewildered. "Don't you know we thought you'd gone off and drowned?"

Joel hung his head.

Again Red came to his rescue. "Let him tell you his

story," he advised. "He didn't do too badly."

"You folks okay here?" Simpson asked.

"Fine, now! Thanks to you people," Marshall told him.

"We better get back then. So long, young Joel." With a casual gesture of farewell, Simpson and Red pulled the raft back into the breaking waves, tumbled into it, and started the motor.

The party on shore waited until the men were taken aboard the cutter. With a farewell hoot the ship got underway.

"Well," Joel's father said. "Let's go up to the kitchen. Joel, we want to hear what you've got to say."

But all the way up the path he kept his arm across Joel's shoulder, so Joel figured he wasn't too mad.

In the kitchen, which was dark because the windows were still boarded over, Marshall Curtis said, "Gary, heat up the coffee."

D.J. said, "Wait a minute! I've got something I've been saving for a special occasion. I think this is it!" She disappeared into the dark lab and came back with a fancy-colored tin. "Fruitcake." She began prying it open with a screwdriver.

"Joel, what would you like to drink?" his father asked.

The unwonted attention embarrassed Joel. "Nothing," he muttered, eyeing the fruitcake.

D.J. gave him the first slice, which was huge.

"Thank God we're all safe," Marshall Curtis said when everyone had cake and those who wanted it had coffee. "Now, Joel, tell us what happened to you."

Joel had been wondering how he could explain Vicky and the eggs without having everyone think he'd lied.

"You remember that day Gary saw a boat and was looking for vandals?" he began.

His father nodded.

"Well, that was Vicky. But she didn't want any grown-ups to see her. She didn't mean me to see her, either, but I did. Anyhow, I promised not to tell. I made her put the eggs back, and she promised not to take any more. It didn't seem so bad to keep it a secret . . ." Joel looked at his father.

"Go on," his father said.

"Then her cousins came to visit us, and I asked them where she was and they said in camp. The next time she came—while I was up at the Mayan Temple—I made her tell me. She'd run away from camp. Nobody wanted her on Owens Island, so she took a boat and was camping on Little Rat." Joel paused to catch his breath.

"Remember that night I saw a light?" Gary exclaimed. "Yes, and you wanted to borrow my boat! I suppose it's good-bye to that."

"No, it's still there, Gary! Honest!" Joel protested.

"But what made you go, when you knew a storm was coming?" his father asked. "I thought you had better sense."

So Joel explained how he thought Sirius had been left behind, and how, if Vicky *was* there, and the hurricane *didn't* come, she'd be mad at Joel for giving away her secret, which was why he'd decided to take a run over there. He told how he'd found Vicky and freed her, how they'd failed to get away from the island, how they'd ridden out the storm and signaled the Coast Guard.

By the time he'd answered all their questions, nothing

remained of the cake but crumbs.

"What a saga!" D.J. summed it up.

Marshall Curtis laughed. "I wouldn't have believed anyone could live a secret life on this island, but Joel's done it!"

Gary decided not to worry about his boat. It would be safe on Little Rat. When the *Bluebell* came, Captain Bell could help him get it.

As it happened, Vicky's father turned up first. Three evenings later he strolled up from the dock. The waters of the Sound were still rough, so his visit surprised everyone.

He introduced himself and said he'd come to thank Joel, and to relay a message from Vicky. She would be out of the hospital in a week, and she hoped Joel would visit her on the island.

"Which island?" Joel asked.

"Owens Island," Vicky's father said.

"You mean she's going to get to stay?" Joel asked.

Under his tan, Mr. Owens' face turned red. "We decided we'd better arrange it," he said. "I'll make my trip later." He looked embarrassed.

"These kids have a way of getting around a person, don't they?" Joel's father said, and both men shook their heads and laughed.

"Did Sirius get home all right?" Joel inquired.

"More spoiled than ever after being entertained at the yacht club."

"You don't have a boat now," Vicky's father remarked on leaving.

"No," Gary said, eyeing Joel.

"As soon as the sea calms down a little more, we'll get over to Little Rat," Vicky's father promised. "Vicky left things there, too, she tells me."

So in due course Gary's boat was retrieved, along with everything else. Little Rat was once again a deserted island.

The time came for Gary and Horace to leave. Their field work with the terns was finished. The birds' breeding season had ended; the colony was dispersing until the following spring. Soon the terns would begin to migrate to South America. No unfledged chicks survived the hurricane, but the older ones did, the ones born early in the season who had already learned to fly.

The night before Gary and Horace left, D.J. and Joel gave a party. Joel even baked another cake. He was afraid, as they all sat laughing and talking over it, that things would be lonesome on Great Rat Island after the next morning.

It turned out that there was so much work to do, with only three of them there, he didn't have time to feel lonesome. Although he did still sometimes wonder about little 995, he was now helping to band a good many other birds. Fall migration was beginning. His father and D.J. and he spent whole days tending the traps and the mist net. They especially hoped to catch a bird already wearing a band.

"Because that's the point of the whole thing," D.J. explained. "It's no good banding them if they're never heard from again. But if a banded bird turns up, we can report its whereabouts this particular August, and the Fish and Wildlife Service will have learned something of its habits and how long it lives. The longest living wild bird we know about was a herring gull. It was found dead on the shore of Lake Michigan. It had been banded in Maine thirty-six years before."

Joel was impressed. "Can you tell that, just from the number?"

"Oh, no. We let the bird go, if it's alive, but we send its number to Washington. The Bird Banding Lab has all the information. Eventually they send you a certificate of appreciation, telling where the bird was banded, and when. The person who banded it gets a report of where it's been found."

"Did you ever get any?"

"Certificates? One. They've received reports here about the terns. That's how we know 'our' terns go to South America."

"I'll bet my father's found some already-banded birds."

"I'll bet he has, too."

But when asked, Marshall Curtis said it didn't matter how many banded birds he'd found. What he wanted was for D.J. and Joel to be lucky this year.

And lucky they were. One afternoon when D.J. and Joel were working together, they found a warbler in the net already wearing a tiny aluminum bracelet. A week later they trapped a banded sandpiper. Joel was allowed to take credit for the sandpiper. The Banding Lab would send the certificate to him.

"I'm going to write about this at school," he told D.J. that evening. "Banding birds and all. Birds don't fly into outer space, but they make very risky flights. It's better than science fiction, because it's true."

He looked up to see his father smiling at him across the table.

16

Picnic on Owens Island

One morning three weeks after the hurricane, Joel stood by the dock and scanned the sea. The morning sun was evaporating the mist. The insects of Great Rat buzzed happily over the weeds. It was a perfect day for a picnic, and Joel was too excited to stand still. He clambered up the hill, shading his eyes, looking for the boat.

He was going to see Vicky for the first time since they'd said good-bye on the Coast Guard cutter. Her father was coming to fetch Joel, Marshall Curtis, and D.J. to Owens Island for the day. And Joel's father had agreed to go; that was the amazing thing.

Vicky's father had come two days ago to invite them. And Marshall Curtis had said, yes, they all deserved a holiday away from Great Rat.

"I guess my father wants to look at osprey nests," Joel said to D.J. when they were alone.

"What makes you think so?" she asked.

Joel frowned thoughtfully. "He doesn't do things just for fun. Remember, he was over there the day we came."

D.J. smiled. "You know something?" she said. "I think he may have changed. That business of the hurricane seems to have humanized him a little."

From the top of the hill Joel saw the boat coming. He ran to summon his father and D.J. and then ran back.

He was waiting on the dock when the cruiser edged alongside. Vicky was standing in the bow, wearing white shorts and a middy. Joel had never seen her so clean. She shouted a greeting and tossed the line. As Joel made it fast, he realized he was doing what he'd watched Horace do six weeks ago. Perhaps not so skillfully, but he wasn't afraid on those narrow planks. He wasn't about to fall, but if he did, it wouldn't matter. He could swim.

Vicky tossed Joel the stern line and then climbed up to join him on the dock. They grinned at each other, while Mr. Owens came back to the after deck to welcome Joel's father and D.J. aboard.

Then they set forth for Vicky's fabulous island, where Captain Kidd had buried his treasure. Today just might be the day they'd find it.